THE OFFICIAL NOVELIZATION

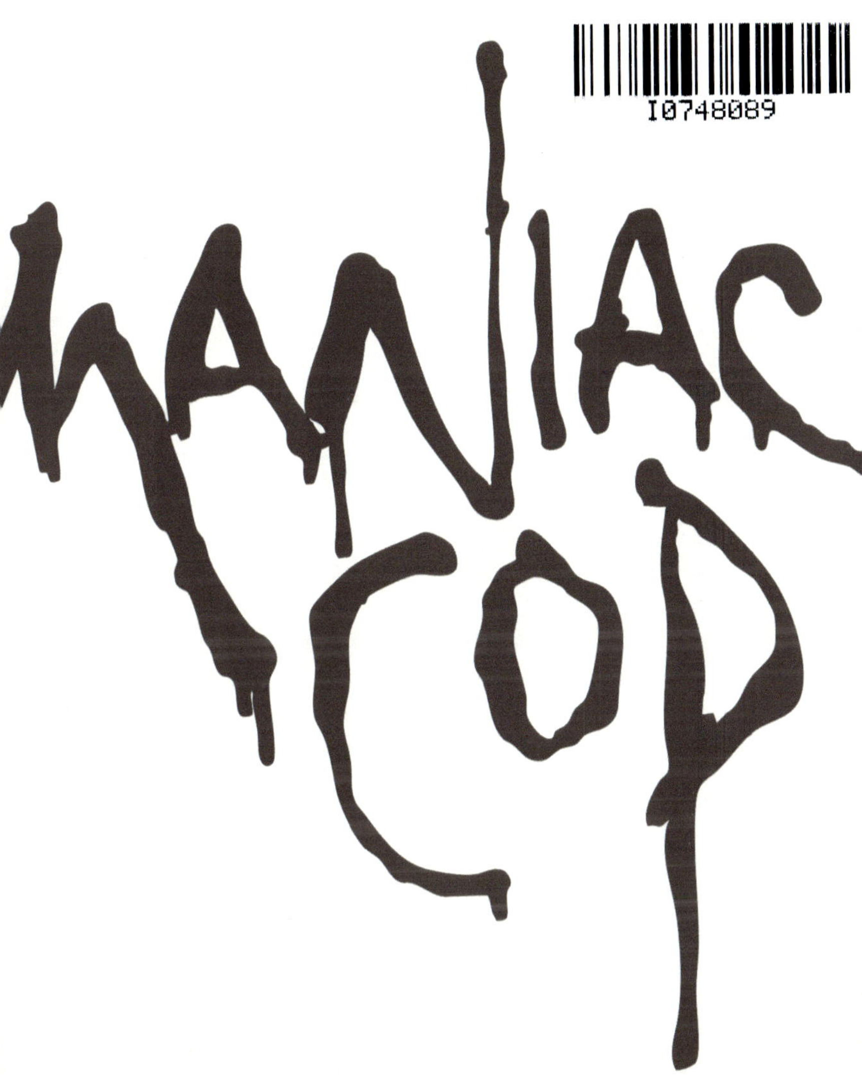

CHRISTIAN FRANCIS

BASED ON THE SCREENPLAY BY LARRY COHEN

ISBN 978-1-916582-70-5 (paperback)
ISBN 978-1-916582-68-2 (ebook)

visit: echohorror.com

Contents

Chapter 1

New York, 1987

By the fourth week of the sanitation workers' strike, the city's trash cans had given way to towering heaps of rotting garbage spilling across sidewalks. With each passing hour, the uncollected waste grew more and more rancid, its stench clawing at anyone unfortunate enough to walk by. Normally, a crisp spring chill might have kept the worst of it at bay, but this year brought an oppressive heatwave instead. The air hung heavy with an unseasonable humidity, which clung to everything and magnified the sour reek of decay that seeped into every crack on the streets . . . and with all this came the rats. Bold and desperate, they tore open the bags of rubbish to feast on moldy fruits, spoiled meats, and other unidentifiable, putrid garbage.

To make matters worse, storm clouds had also

rolled in, dark and swollen with the promise of release. But instead of breaking and washing the heat and stink away, they loomed, motionless, trapping the sweltering city in a new suffocation that made it feel like a pressure cooker. Every passerby seemed more on edge than normal, somehow more dangerous as a simmering anger threatened to explode from them. Drivers punched their horns with casual ease, even at the most innocuous of annoyances. Pedestrians shouted their curses freely, fists raised in defiance at other people, at the trash, at the unrelenting humidity, at *anything*. The storm wasn't just in the sky; it was here in the streets, in the air, in each person. It felt raw and stripped down to the bone. It felt like the city could smell blood and was about to snap.

This was even more true in lower Manhattan, especially on the streets, where the Lost Dog Tavern sat. As bums and junkies wandered aimlessly through the night, Cassie Phillips, a twenty-year-old barmaid, walked out the tavern's exit, wearing her usual short ruffled skirt and high heels. She hurriedly put on her raincoat as she stared up at the clouds. She had hoped the storm would have arrived by then, but instead, the pressure just gave her a headache she'd had to endure for the past few days.

"Come on, Cass," a patron of the bar slurred at her as he stumbled out behind her, inebriated from his night's excesses. "I know an after-hours joint. I'll get ya some booze. Ya need it. You been on your feet long enough."

"Forget it." Cassie smirked, familiar with these kinds of proposals from her clientele. "I got a day job, too, ya know?" Turning to the man, she offered him a smile. "Get home safe, okay? You should get some sleep, too."

"Safe? Me? Nah, it's you who's gotta be safe. I should give you a lift." The man's voice became increasingly drunken as the night air slapped his lungs. "You don't wanna be walking round here alone, do ya?"

Shaking her head, Cassie smiled as she started off up the street. "I'd rather fight off the muggers than chance you driving."

With a chuckle, the patron quickly disappeared back into the closing tavern, with the hope to find anyone else who may join him in his continued revelry.

Adjusting her handbag more firmly on her shoulder, Cassie carried on up the street with a confident stride. She had a good night, despite the headache, having flirted enough with the grotesque locals of the Lost Dog to get herself a nice haul of tips. All she had to do was smile and ignore their hands as she served them their overpriced, watered-down booze. She hated every one of those people and would like nothing more than to punch them in the balls every time they pinched her ass or stroked her arm or mumbled incoherent obscenities they *thought* were compliments. Instead, she smiled and took their money, making sure to short-change them and keep the difference. She saw that as a win. A gross, uncomfortable win.

As her heels clacked on the sidewalk, she turned up a side street leading to Alphabet City. She had been told by her boss on many occasions not to walk home alone, but as she saw it, she was no wallflower, and the small gun in her handbag would protect her enough from anyone stupid enough to corner her.

Anyway, just as she had every other night, she arrived home without incident as she saw the familiar, converted brownstone just up ahead.

She walked with purpose, rummaging in her pocket for her keys, unaware of the shadows that flitted behind her. One crossed from an alley to a car behind her. Another was on the opposite side of the street, and the third was slowly following her, keeping its distance. Like in a jungle, these things were approaching like predators, silently moving so as to not alert their prey.

Grabbing her house keys, Cassie suddenly heard a loud clang of metal coming from her left, which made her hold her breath and stop in her tracks.

Cautiously glancing around, she gripped her keys tight, ready to use them as a weapon in case she had no time to reach for her gun.

A trash can rolled on the sidewalk, having been knocked over.

She then saw the culprits, a pack of alley cats tearing away from the scene as the loud noise of the falling bin scared them.

With a smirk, Cassie turned back to carry on to her apartment.

"Hey there, mi amor!" a leering voice said with a gleeful menace.

In front of her, two skinny men stood in her path. Both were obvious junkies, who looked her up and down hungrily. Their clothes were filthy and threadbare, their skin dirt stained, their arms littered with bruised track marks, their bodies emaciated.

"What you got for us?" the other said viciously through gritted teeth.

Cassie was a city girl through and through. She would not relent to this kind of intimidation.

"You think I'm gonna give you assholes squat?" she said, unafraid.

Before she could say anymore, one of the junkies lunged at her. "Puta!"

But he did not see Cassie's heavy handbag swing through the air straight toward him. The leather smacked the junkie on the side of the head heavily as he fell to the side, into his friend, dazed.

Cassie didn't wait for round two. She quickly darted down the narrow alley, running beside the brownstone, frantically scanning for a fire escape ladder. Usually, these were left lowered, but that night, inexplicably, every ladder was raised, cutting off her planned escape.

"Dammit," she seethed.

As she looked up to the windows above, she could

see they were all shut with the apartment lights off. No one seemed to be home in the whole building.

Hurrying farther into the alley, over a wash of fallen trash, Cassie suddenly lost her footing as one of her heels slipped on some slimy detritus. It painfully buckled beneath her, sending her forward onto a nearby metal dumpster. She yelped as her arm twisted, and scraped on the dumpster's rusty rim.

Getting to her feet, she forced herself onward, ignoring the pain. She had to get out of there. The alley was dark and menacing enough at night, but with the threat of the junkies, it was terrifying. She had to think fast. She chided herself silently for even coming down here.

She glanced around, looking for any way to escape. In front of her, a fenced-off part of the next-door building was currently in the early stages of being demolished. And to her side, a looming brick wall.

Slowly turning, Cassie had expected to see the two men approaching her like hungry hyenas, but the alley was still. Had her handbag hit scared them off? With a relieved sigh, she smiled.

Opening her handbag, she went for her gun. The junkies may not be in her view, but they could still be hiding somewhere. Before she could grab the hilt, one of the junkies suddenly screamed in anger as he leaped over the fence. Narrowly missing her, he fell hard onto the concrete.

Cassie whirled and hurried as fast as her heels

would allow her, back up the alley toward the street. But she soon saw the silhouette of the other junkie at the entrance, waiting for her. Though she could not see his face, she could see one thing; the small knife in his hand, the metal glinting at her from a nearby streetlight.

There was only one way she could go, up a narrow break between a neighboring building and the demolition site.

She darted toward it, hearing the junkies yelling in pursuit.

"¡Regresa aquí, perra!" one of them shrieked in a fury.

Above, in one of the buildings, a light switched on as an old man peered out to see what was causing the commotion. He could plainly see the two men in the alley chasing Cassie.

"You little motherfuckers," he screamed to them with a voice that sounded like it was made of gravel. "Leave her alone, or I'll call the cops! I see ya, ya pissants!"

As she ran, Cassie fumbled, trying to grab her gun from her handbag. But in her panic, she suddenly lost her grip, and her bag tumbled to the ground. She could not stop running. She could hear the men behind her, cackling and whooping with a perverse glee. She had to leave the gun.

In a panic, she glanced over her shoulder to see how close her attackers were, how close she was to something awful happening, but she did not see the large figure step into the path in front of her.

Before she could turn back, she collided with a navy blue dressed figure. A huge presence that did not even budge as she ran into it. All this man did was raise his hand and grip her by the shoulder, steadying her.

With a gasp, Cassie's terrified expression shifted to relief as she stared up at this huge man. "Thank God!"

The man was clearly a cop, who stood nearly seven feet tall in his beat uniform.

Cassie did not even notice the white gloves he wore. The white gloves that police only wore for ceremonial duties. Nor did she see his face under his eight-point cap as thick shadows cloaked him.

All she saw was the bright silver badge on his chest.

"They nearly got me," she said, motioning to the alley behind her.

The junkies were gone.

"I dropped my purse. I . . . Couldn't . . ." As she turned back to the officer, her words fell from her mouth. She realized that his gloved hand was still gripping her shoulder, and he was not saying a thing to her. "Aren't you going to do anything?"

With his free hand, this cop then reached inside his buttoned jacket and pulled out a long, thick stiletto knife.

Cassie stared at the blade in shock. She could not fathom what was happening. Why would a policeman carry a knife like this? Or why he would bring it in front of her now? Not unless . . .

She felt the grip on her shoulder tighten.

"No," she whimpered. "Please . . . I didn't do anything."

The man raised the knife, ready to strike.

As he did, the two junkies had approached and picked up Cassie's fallen bag. But instead of running away with their haul, they just stood, frozen, in witness ahead of them.

Both junkies had seen a lot on these streets. They had done a lot. They thought they had seen everything. But they watched, feeling a cold terror seep over them.

Cassie screamed as the cop then yanked her back, gripping her against him, turning her, so she faced the junkies. A ribbon of light shone down from a security light nearby and traced over Cassie's petrified expression.

"Help me!" she cried out to her pursuers.

Knowing what was gripping her was the worst of the two evils in this alley.

The blade then came crashing down with a tremendous force and into Cassie's stomach.

She had expected agony, but there wasn't any. Instead, she just felt a chilling numbness in her belly. A cold so sharp it made her even more petrified. The second and third stabs were the same. Then came the pain and then the realization that this was the end.

As the junkies scrambled away in a panic, they

could hear Cassie's gurgled screams in the distance. They did not want to look back as they ran but could not help themselves. They watched in frenzied glances as the goliath cop brought the knife down over and over again into Cassie's body. An unrelenting assault of repeated violence.

As her legs gave way and her heart stopped beating, the cop still held onto her tightly, stabbing.

Less than an hour later, that same alleyway was awash with yellow and blue light as the NYPD cordoned it off and examined the crime scene.

One of the junkies stood at the far end, handcuffed as an officer held him by the arm. Another officer stood close by, Cassie's bag in his latex gloved hands as he looked inside, searching evidence.

The junkie was panicked, staring at where the attack happened. Unable to peel his eyes from it. "Yeah, yeah, we took the bag from her," he said. "But we didn't touch her. We didn't kill her, man. I swear it wasn't us!"

"And who did, huh?" the officer searching the bag asked with an annoyed grunt. "Jimmy Hoffa? Bigfoot?"

"It was a cop, man!" the junkie almost screamed out. "It wasn't us! It was a damn cop!"

The officer holding him pushed the junkie up against the nearby wall. "Shut the fuck up before I shut you up," he seethed. "Don't go blaming us. We protect your dumbasses."

"I'm telling you!" the junkie cried in hysterics. "He was *huge*. Had a cuchillo. A big ass knife! Dude was crazy! My buddy'll say the same!"

"And I'll ask him when they bring him in."

———

Detective Lieutenant Frank McCrae was standing in the police mortuary, looking down at the remains of Cassie Phillips on the cold, metal table. Frank was a craggy, handsome man in his fifties. He was hard-drinking, hard-working, and hard to not like. With graying hair and a thin mustache, he looked at least a decade older than he actually was. A policeman for over three decades, he had gone from patrolling skid row and busting wannabe gangbangers to hunting the drug lords, murderers, and rapists—all the worst elements of New York. Over his time on the force, he had seen the worst of what humans could do to one another, yet he still held out hope that there was good in everyone. Somewhere.

As he stared down at Cassie's naked, mutilated remains on the slab, he could not help but feel angry. Her stomach and chest were ripped open so far that it looked less like a multitude of knife wounds and instead like a huge ax had attacked her. He glanced at her pale, blank face. He would have loved to have thought that she died quickly and without pain but could tell, from the bruising, that her final moments were as agonizing as they were terrifying.

"You seriously are trying to tell that this damage was done with a switchblade?" he asked. "You really believe that?"

"We got a statement from a guy in the apartments," Detective Lovejoy replied. "He saw those tweakers chasing her with switchblades." Fixing his eyes intently on Frank, Lovejoy was anxious to not see any of this dead body. Squeamish at even the sight of blood, he knew it would have sent his lunch straight back up should he have focused on it.

A few years younger than Frank, Lovejoy did the work he was asked to do, but that was all. He was analytical and at his best just looking at facts. Not trawling the backstreets and being close to the blood. In his own words, he was a "nerd with a gun."

"So, what more do you want—" Lovejoy continued as he suddenly stopped. Feeling his stomach churn, he had caught sight of Cassie's wound out of his periphery. "Can someone cover that up?" he asked to a mortician standing by. "It's fucking gross."

"Her name's Cassie Phillips. Not *that*," Frank snapped.

Lovejoy raised his eyebrow at the comment. Frank always felt empathy, but to Lovejoy, this seemed too harsh a reaction. Then a creeping realization came over him, followed by a truckload of guilt. It was clear in his expression that Frank actually knew this woman.

On the other side of the table, silently observing, Assistant District Attorney Peter Harper, stood, looking as surprised as Lovejoy.

Frank sighed. "I used to stop at the Lost Dog for a nightcap," he said, looking mournfully at Cassie's face. "She always had the best jokes. So damn funny, that girl. I told her over and over that she should go to The Comedy Cellar and try some stand-up."

"All the more reason you should listen to me, and we should lock those dopeheads up," Lovejoy said, still averting his gaze. "Now, please, can we pull a sheet over her? It's too much."

"Don't pass out on me, Lovejoy." Frank smirked painfully. "No, look at the wounds."

"Come on," Lovejoy complained, still averting his gaze.

"Cassie was five-ten. And she had four-inch heels on."

"She was big. So what?"

Lovejoy had had enough. He wanted out. Even the smell of the formaldehyde offended his nostrils.

"So, whoever did this slashed downward from above. We can see that from the angle of the wound. And it was done over and over with a shit ton of force. So, the person had to have been taller than her, right? And the tweaker's blades were too thin to do this much damage. *And* neither of them had a drop of her blood on them."

Lovejoy started to see what was being proposed. Something he didn't like to hear. A moment ago, it was a shut case. The junkies banged to rights. But it was opening up again.

"The guy who did this had to have been well over six-eight to even get that angle. Maybe bigger." Frank's eyes moved from Cassie up to Lovejoy. "And what were those kids? Five-six at a push? Maybe it is exactly as they said?"

"You think it's a cop? Really, Frank?" Lovejoy turned to the still silent Harper incredulously. "You aren't buying this bull, too, are ya?"

Harper shrugged.

"Why not?" Frank shrugged. "She knew me. She knew a lot of cops. Not out of the realm of possibility here that one could do this. Out of all the NYPD, there has gotta be one rotten apple."

Lovejoy shook his head. He could not believe Frank was entertaining what two high on junk kids said. "Let's just get out of here. I need some fresh air." Without waiting, he turned and left the room, trying his best to suppress his present nausea.

"You really believe it could be one of us?" Harper asked, finally speaking up after Lovejoy had left.

"Ah, I dunno," Frank replied. "I've no clue but can't just dismiss it 'cause I don't like it."

"Well, I got a ruling from the commissioner on all

this. No one speaks a word about the case. Not to anyone outside the department. Not your friends or family. No one. They don't want this getting out. Okay?"

With that, Harper left the room. Not even waiting for a confirmation of the order.

As the door slammed, Frank turned his attention back to Cassie. Nodding to the attendant mortician, he watched as a white sheet was pulled up over her.

"Sorry I wasn't there to save you," Frank muttered softly. "You must've been so scared and then . . . you saw a cop . . ."

———

The next night as the clock hit 3 a.m., once again, the bars in lower Manhattan were closing. The storm clouds above still refused to break as the sweatiness in the city persisted. Once again, the drunks and party people were ejected from their revelry and were starting to drift home.

Through these downtown streets, a beaten-up Buick swerved. Behind its wheel, Sam Amerson tried to focus on the street ahead as he laughed in hysterics. Aged twenty-two, he was having the best time. He was also far above the legal limit as he reached over to Nancy Ellis, his girlfriend, and took the beer from her offering hand. Taking a swig, he handed the bottle back to her. She was in no state to tell him to not drink and drive, being in the same condition he was.

From the radio, an almost deafening volume of pop music screamed out of the speakers as he drove haphazardly, attempting to stay in the correct lane through his blurry vision.

"I think we just about closed that club," he laughed.

"We're hardcore, plain and simple." Nancy grinned back. But her smile quickly dropped as she pointed ahead of them. "Watch it! There's a light turning."

"Ah, I see it." Sam shrugged dismissively, pumping on the brake.

The car soon stopped, with a slight skid ahead of a line in the street. The light to his side red, brightly blaring into the night.

For a few moments, Sam looked at the intersection around him. There was no one around. They were at this light, stopped for no other traffic.

More moments passed, and the light remained red.

Sam stared up at it through the windshield, willing for the light to turn. "What's up with that thing?" he said, holding out his hand for the beer.

Passing it over, Nancy looked around the streets. "Seems silly having lights for no cars."

Sam nodded, taking a sip.

Nancy continued. "What's the rush, anyway? Not like we got plans."

Leaning over the seat toward him, she took the bottle back and nuzzled up to his neck. "We could do it right here and now, and no one would even know."

A smile crept upon Sam's face as he turned to her excitedly.

Their flirtation was quickly cut short by a sharp rapping upon the roof of the car.

Quickly turning out the driver's side window, Sam couldn't see down the street, which was blocked by the body of a cop standing outside. A cop who had pounded on the roof to get their attention.

"Ditch the beer," Sam whispered. "It's a damn cop."

"Where did he come from?" Nancy asked as she tucked the beer bottle under the seat.

With a shrug, Sam rolled down his window and put on a large smile, masking his drunkenness as best as he could. "Hello, Officer. What's seems to be the trouble?"

No reply.

From inside the car, the music still blared.

"I think he wants you to get out," Nancy said.

Before Sam could answer, the cop reached out its white-gloved hand and opened the driver-side door.

Sam looked shocked. "What the—"

"You better cooperate," Nancy said. "Don't give them any reason."

"Fuck," Sam muttered as he unclasped his seat belt and got out of the car.

As he did, his foot clipped another empty beer bottle that had been stuffed into the driver's door pocket. It clinked loudly onto the street in front of the cop.

Sheepishly and with an annoyed groan, Sam got out and picked up the bottle from the floor. "It was just one beer, Officer," Sam lied, handing over the bottle. "Totally legal to have one, right?"

The cop's gloved hand reached out and took the bottle from him.

"I've never done anything wrong before," Sam continued, babbling in panic. "If I did anything wrong, please tell me, and I'm sure I can make it right." He closed the driver's door behind him, and the loud song instantly muffled.

Inside the car, Nancy tried to hear what was being said but was too afraid to turn down the music and draw attention to herself. She could only sit as she watched the cop motion to the front of the car, where Sam obediently followed.

In the glare of their headlights, Sam then walked a straight line on the street. Touching his fingertips together. A rudimentary sobriety text that the large cop mimed for Sam to do.

Nancy tried to see the cop's face, but with his back to her and the silhouetting of the lights, she could not make out what she thought she had seen. She could have sworn this man had something on his face. A wound or some deformity. For a brief second as he had walked Sam around, she had caught a glimpse, and it scared her.

Blocking her view of Sam, there was little Nancy could do.

Then, the cop lunged forward with a sudden snap. His shoulders moved as he was doing something out of Nancy's view.

She slid over to the driver's side to get a better look, but it did not help.

Before she could realize what had happened, the cop turned and violently hurled Sam's dying body at the windshield.

As he was grabbed and wrestled by the huge cop, Sam had felt each of his ribs breaking inward as this man's enormous arms battered down on him. He felt his spine snapping, his thigh bones shatter, his skull crack. He was beaten with a terrible strength in the space of a few seconds. The agony he felt was beyond description as his nerves burned. The next thing he felt was the beer bottle being slammed into his mouth, cracking his teeth inward as it was rammed down into his throat.

The car's windshield shattered inward as Sam's body smashed into it. The force of the impact was so immense his body was pushed through the jagged glass at incredible speed. And as it was, his skin had been sliced back and his flesh torn apart, causing torrents of dark blood to spray out into the car, across the glass and over Nancy.

Sam's dying eyes met Nancy's, the bottle lodged in his broken mouth as he let out a terrible muffled gargle of agony. His body then began to convulse.

With a hideous scream, Nancy stared at her boyfriend's twitching, dying remains, then out to the street. Through the cracked and bloody glass, she could see that the cop was no longer standing in front of the car.

Above, the light finally flicked green. Like it was her permission to run, Nancy suddenly slammed the car into drive and hit the gas.

As the car lurched across the intersection, Sam's lifeless body slid inside, through the hole in the windshield. It collapsed in a bloodied heap half on the passenger seat and half on Nancy, who could not stop screaming.

Chapter 2

Commissioner James Pike was a slippery weasel of a man. A red-faced ex-cop who reveled in city politics, an arena he played in masterfully, bending it to serve his every ambition. As the head of the police force, a role he savored with unabashed relish, Pike demanded obedience from his subordinates, whether they respected him or not. And none did.

Frank McCrae, in particular, hated that man. Pike made Frank's skin crawl. So much so that Frank often called Pike "the leech" to others. He saw the commissioner as a bloodsucker who did not care who he destroyed to get what he wanted.

"You're just casually assuming this was a police officer?" Pike asked, stone-faced. "What about a nutjob dressed as a cop?"

Frank shrugged. "Yeah, it could be someone

dressing up. But with the girlfriend in the car's statement, it's definitely not those junkies."

"It's not one of us. You can wipe that from your head. It screams out one message loudly," Pike said with a self-satisfied grin. "Says to me that this guy wants to discredit the force. It fits into my profile to the T. He's not a cop. He's trying to frame us. Playing dress-up as he kills. And we *can't* let it get out that he's in uniform. We can't let him win."

"All the same, I think we better not discount that it could be NYPD," Frank said. "I gotta say, though, my hunch say that it's one of us."

"Oh, you have a hunch, do you?" Pike replied with derision. "And hunches beats evidence now, do they?"

"Hasn't steered me wrong so far." Frank smiled before pivoting. "Either way, pretender or real, we should get the police psychologist to give us a rundown on any officers they think could do this. Anyone assessed that might be unstable. May have tried suicide or been under emotional pressure or with a history of violence. We can't just stop looking inward 'cause we don't like that it. Or discount a testimony because the people telling it are assholes. Those junkies said it was a real cop. We should at least consider it."

Pike regarded him with a curious amusement. He found the kind of cop Frank was, hilarious. The kind who thought that they could fix what had always been broken. The do-gooder.

"Why don't we give the *entire* force a sanity check while we're at it?" Pike smirked.

"It's not the *entire* force. We're looking for a White male, well over six feet tall, without an alibi for those nights. It's hardly a huge pool of people to look at. What can it hurt, anyway?" Frank paused as he glared at Pike. "And, yeah, it could be someone playing cop, but what if it isn't? Doing this will show you gave all lines of inquiry the same attention . . . without any bias."

The commissioner's expression dropped. Frank's words were barbed and hit their target exactly. Previously in the press, Pike had been accused of class and racial bias in some of the higher-profile investigations he oversaw. He did not want another article accusing him of anything like that. Though he didn't want to, he felt compelled to comply with Frank's request, no matter how ridiculous it sounded to him. Anything to try and avert any focus of the newspapers being on him again.

"Okay, run with your psych tests," Pike sighed. "But my order still stands. I want this cop stuff kept on the strict QT. Not a single word gets out about any uniform. Not to anyone."

"Keep it quiet? Why? For how long? The public should be told to be on the lookout. To look beyond the badge," Frank said. "He'll kill again. He obviously enjoys doing it and—"

"We can't have *any*one think it's us. It'll be a media

shitstorm if they do. We can't have anyone turning on the NYPD, real or imagined."

Frank knew Pike was right in that it would be bad for the force if anyone suspected a cop, but his only focus was saving lives, nothing else. Certainly not how anyone saw him.

"You seem to know a lot about this guy, don't you, McCrae?" Pike added with a sneer. "Maybe *you* should be first on the shrink's couch?"

"Anytime, sir. I'm not hiding anything." Frank smiled.

He would not be riled. He would not allow Pike the satisfaction of seeing any of his words affect him.

Pike didn't relent. "Well, you're the one who tried to shoot himself a couple of years back, aren't ya? That's some emotional pressure right there. *That's* unstable. Makes you a prime suspect, doesn't it?"

Frank stared back blankly. "The gun went off. It wasn't intentional."

"Sure, sure, ten days after your partner was killed in the line of duty. Your gun miraculously discharged itself, *at you.*"

"What are you implying with this, Commissioner?"

Pike smiled. "I'm not implying anything, Detective. I'm stating facts. You fit your threadbare profile."

"I'm not over six-three. And I have alibis."

"Fine, you fit *most* of your threadbare profile," Pike replied, shaking his head. "You don't seem in any better state of mind since your gun 'went off.' You never smile. So, you really should be first suspect in line for being looked at."

Frank, as if on command, smiled a broad fake smile at the commissioner. One that was devoid of any joy or humor and more like an animal baring its teeth.

Pike motioned to the door. "Now, get out. And not a word from anyone about this suspect. No mention of a uniform."

———

Along 52nd Street, the parade of jazz clubs—which had been alive just an hour before, with smoky, sultry sounds of swing and the electric energy of a packed crowd blaring out onto the street—they all lay silent and in darkness. The music that poured from their doors and windows had faded, the entrances had been bolted shut, and their glowing neon signs were switched off. The streets they were on were left in a hollow silence.

From the side entrance of The Cadence Club, Eddie Baker stepped out into the sticky night. His double bass, encased in a scuffed, zip-up cover, was slung over his shoulder, its bulk weighing down on him as much as the long evening's playing had. He adjusted the strap and sighed as he took a moment to breathe in the night air. With the added stench of trash that permeated, it was still better than the thick smoke that he had inhaled all night from the baying club crowds.

Behind him, a handful of fellow musicians trickled out, one by one, their instruments tucked under arms or rolling in battered cases. They exchanged their quiet nods and murmured farewells.

"Later, Baker," one called over his shoulder, his voice hoarse but friendly as that group turned to walk in the opposite direction toward the Hudson River.

As the others said similar goodbyes, their tones blended into a low rumble of tired but amicable grunts.

"See ya on the flip side, fellas," Eddie called out with a wave, his voice weary.

He turned down the narrow side street, his strap digging into his shoulder as he trudged toward his car, parked just a couple of blocks ahead. The streetlamps around him flickered faintly, casting their long shadows as he walked by. The distant clatter of garbage cans and the faint rustle of a breeze through the alleys accompanied his journey. It was the sound of a city that never truly slept but still managed to rest between beats. This was Eddie's favorite time of night.

Six days a week, he would leave the club at the same time, bid the same farewells to his comrades and walk the same path to his car. And every night, he would listen to the sound of the resting city around him. There was rarely anyone else around at this time, not this far across town. Maybe the occasional prostitute on her way home or dealer looking for a new buyer but nothing else. So, when he got to his car and popped the trunk, he was surprised when he noticed a cop on the corner watching him from a nearby alley.

Swinging his instrument off his shoulder, he placed it into the trunk and smiled at the cop. "I'm not ripping nothing off, Officer," he called over loudly. "This is my car. Got the pink slip in the glove box if you wanna see?"

The cop stepped out from the alley and moved across the sidewalk to him.

Eddie noticed, with some confusion, the dress gloves this large policeman wore. "Been somewhere fancy, Officer?" he asked with a smirk, but he quickly noticed the cop reaching for the handcuffs on his belt. "Shit, you wanna see my cabaret license? Or my union card? Let's not let this get out of hand!"

The cop held up his handcuffs open, ready to be snapped on a wrist.

Eddie stared at this cop, trying to see his face, trying to see someone he could charm or bargain with. But thick shadows covered this man as the streetlight behind only silhouetted him.

"Come on, buddy," Eddie pleaded. "Don't arrest me, I haven't done diddly squat."

The cop jangled the handcuffs menacingly, and with his other hand, he pointed a finger out and made a circular motion, signifying for Eddie to turn around.

"Okay, fine," Eddie complied, turning around and raising his hands but not liking it one bit. Knowing better than to get on the wrong side of a cop. "Take me in if you gotta, but I've done nothin' wrong. They'll just let me out again."

The click of the handcuffs locking reverberated around this quiet backstreet as Eddie was forcefully manacled, then spun back around to face the cop.

This close, the shadows broke over the officer's face, and Eddie could clearly see him. This man's heavily butchered face.

"Jesus," Eddie gasped as his eyes traced over the scars of the man towering above him. "What the hell happened to you?"

Without a word, the cop reached down to his belt and unclipped his large billy club.

Eddie's eyes widened in fear, then grew confused as the cop did not hold the club as a weapon but instead started to unscrew its handle.

His wooden weapon came apart as the large portion of the club lifted off to reveal the long stiletto knife below it, his club acting as a disguised sheath for the blade. A blade which still had dulling of redness over it, that Eddie could see in the streetlight's glow was dried blood.

"No," Eddie whispered in fear as his eyes quickly darted up and down the street, hoping to see another person.

A witness. A savior. Anyone. But this was not a residential neighborhood. It was all stores, businesses, and clubs, and at this early in the morning, no one was around.

Before Eddie could turn and run, the cop thrust his broad hand firmly against Eddie's chest, sending him stumbling several steps up the street. Without a word, the cop lifted his hand again, dismissing him with a curt shooing motion.

Eddie stared in alarm. "You're letting me go?" he said as his voice trembled. "You're playin' with me, right?"

His gaze then flicked to the blade, clenched tightly in the cop's hand. Realizing just how dangerous this situation had become, how dangerous this cop was, he felt his desperation take over.

"Help!" Eddie suddenly yelled, his voice cracking. "For God's sake, someone help me! Please!"

But these cries echoed emptily around him. He turned to run but didn't know which way. His gaze then shifted back to the cop, bracing himself for the worst, knowing all too well the history of encounters like this. He fully expected this monstrous figure to carry out what had been done to Black people, time and time again, in this country, a grim, unchanging reality.

But the cop was gone.

Eddie's breath became ragged as he tried to see where the officer went. Fighting the rising panic within him.

Knowing his hands were firmly handcuffed behind

him, making driving away impossible, Eddie immediately did the only thing he could think of. He turned and ran, just as the cop has motioned for him to do.

His leather shoes clacking beneath him, Eddie sprinted with all his might back up the side street, toward a more populated part of town. Then he saw it, the door to The Cadence Club he had exited not too long ago. Throwing himself up against the handless back door, he slammed his body against it, unable to free his hands to knock.

"Open up," he yelled. Hoping that someone in the club was still inside, cleaning or cashing up. "There's a crazy cop! Someone open up! Help me!"

Pausing for a moment, not hearing someone coming from the club to answer his call, he, instead, heard heavy, determined footsteps on the sidewalk behind him, getting closer by the second.

"Get the fuck away from me!" Eddie screamed. Without glancing back or waiting a second longer for the door to open, he pivoted sharply and tore across the street. Racing, his footsteps took over the sounds of the night, louder than anything else around him.

"Help!" he screamed as he darted toward the entrance of another club across the street.

It was just as shadowed and locked as The Cadence Club, but his desperation forced him. Slamming his heel against the glass panel door, he felt it crack and buckle under the force. As it did, the blaring of a burglar alarm immediately pierced the air. For the first time, he welcomed that noise. It was louder than his own cries had been, and maybe—just *maybe*—someone would hear it.

"Someone, anyone! Help!" he cried out again, his voice growing hoarser. With the alarm shrieking and without hesitation, he didn't want to wait, so he turned and sprinted farther down the street, leaving the shattered door behind him.

Turning a corner, his eyes soon landed on a large brownstone, a block of apartments next to a line of vacant stores. He pushed forward, his heart pounding like a drum.

Scampering up the steps, almost losing his balance from his hands still tied, he reached for the panel of buzzers. He quickly began pushing the buzzers with his nose. Any and all of them he could depress. The old solid buttons were stiff and hurt, but he had no choice.

"Hurry, please," he muttered in a panic. "Answer. Come on, come on, come on."

The speaker was silent for a few excruciating moments until a static buzzed out. Someone was answering, and Eddie's face lit up.

"What the hell d'you want?" an extremely annoyed woman asked. "You know what damn time it is?"

"Help me," Eddie blurted. "There's a psycho cop after me. He got a knife. Tried to kill me. Please, buzz me in. Please."

Expecting to hear the door unlocking, he instead heard a moan of annoyance from the woman on the speaker.

"Fuck off. Or I'll call the cops."

With an annoyed grunt, Eddie turned away. What else could he have expected. Bounding down the steps, he raced farther down the street.

His eyes soon fixed on a nearby construction site, a maze of scaffolding and half-finished structures. *If I could cut through it*, he thought, *I might be able to reach Chinatown.* It was only a few blocks away, and Eddie knew that part of the city never truly shut down. He clung to the hope that someone could be there to help him.

As he moved toward the site, his focus wavered just long enough to miss the jagged edge of a curb where the sidewalk had been torn up for replacing. His toe caught painfully against the concrete, forcing his leg backward. The momentum of his body carried him forward. With his arms uselessly bound, he hurtled headlong into the wet, freshly poured cement in front of him with a sticky thud.

Before he could squirm his way out, a jarring force then hit the back of his head, pressing down on him with an unrelenting pressure, driving his face deeper into the cement. As his ears submerged in the thick slurry, muffling the world around him, his mouth filled with the foul, gritty mixture, and his chin hit the rough dirt beneath.

Eddie tried to scream, but the solidifying sludge smothered his sounds as each futile flail of his limbs had become weaker than the last. He fought desperately, his legs kicking and body twisting in a frantic resistance, but the force on the back of his head was immovable, a cold and merciless anchor that pinned him down. His mind raced, trying to grasp this new reality. But as the thick, bitter cement crept farther into his airways, his thoughts darkened and his body started to spasm. Once. Then again. Then once more . . . until finally, he was still.

Above as he sheathed the stiletto knife back into its billy club, the large cop removed his heavy boot from the back of Eddie's lifeless head.

A few hours later, the gloom of night had given way to an overcast morning. As the city stirred awake, a passerby noticed something unusual on their way to work, a figure partially encased in hardened cement. Eddie, in mid-struggle, lifeless and face down, locked in his final moments. Soon after, the police had arrived on the scene, bringing some construction workers along with them. Armed with pickaxes and drills, these men had busily begun working to get Eddie's body free. Trying to chip away at his half-visible grave as delicately as they could.

They would not have tied it to the other murders had it have not been for what the large cop did to

Eddie's body after. His whole back had been brutally and repeatedly stabbed into one open massive wound. Attacked with such aggression that his spine had been cracked inward from the weight of the stabbing.

———

Hell's Kitchen sat a mile away. It was one of the few places Frank McCrae felt safe in this city. Despite its name, Hell's Kitchen was a place for family. It was where hard-working immigrants moved after arriving in America, just as his parents had. Sure, it was poor, but unlike the rest of New York, it was not a place of drugs and gangs. The only crime here was from old-school families who made sure that no innocent people ever got involved in their dealings. Even the criminals had morals here. At least that was Frank's rose-tinted view of it all.

Sitting in Jake's Saloon, a hangout for cops since the start of the twentieth century, at a booth in the far corner, Frank sat cradling a glass of cheap bourbon in his hand. After three drinks in, the cheap liquor burned his throat pleasingly. Checking the clock on the wall, he saw it read 4:55 p.m. He had five minutes to go until his meeting. He looked at the remaining half-measure in his glass and considered getting a fourth-round in.

"Heya, Frank," a man said, stealing Frank's attention from his glass.

Standing at the edge of the booth was Tom Shepard, a veteran newsman who wore a rumpled trench coat and carried a scuffed leather satchel over his shoulder. His graying hair pushed back in uneven waves, framed his puffy face. Thick glasses rested on his bulbous nose, and a cigarette dangled from his lips.

"Am I early?" Tom asked with a surprised smile. "I swore I'd be late. They had me taping a special feature for the eleven o'clock."

"Five minutes to spare." Frank grinned. "I'm impressed!"

Tom removed his satchel and sat down opposite.

"What was the special feature?" Frank asked.

Tom sighed. "Those sons a bitches are back across Harlem, selling crack." He shook his head. "Thought we chased them off already. But these new gangs are bold as brass with no damn class."

"Well, I got a better story for you." Frank grinned again.

"How stiff a drink do I need?"

Frank turned and lifted his glass without replying, effortlessly catching the bartender's eye. Raising two fingers in a quiet gesture, he offered a faint, knowing smile. The bartender nodded, understanding the order.

"That bad?" Tom asked, not needing to be told anymore. "Then again, I'm not surprised. In twenty years of knowing you, you know how many stories you've leaked to me?"

Frank shrugged knowingly.

"None. Nada. Zero. Zilch." Tom then smiled. "You're a good friend, but you're the most tight-lipped bastard I ever met. What changed?"

"Three homicides. Same perp. City covering it all up to save face."

The bartender then appeared, placed two glasses of bourbon on their table, then retreated to the bar.

Tom quickly took a sip from his glass. "I hope you're not gonna tell me it's another Son of Sam. Dunno if my heart could take that."

Frank took a breath in, and as his smile dropped, Tom could tell it was probably worse.

"Dammit, Frank," Tom continued. "How bad could it be?"

"The worst," Frank replied gravely. "This one's a cop."

Tom's expression sagged. "You gotta be shittin' me."

"Cop with a knife," Frank continued. "Got witnesses, and the commissioner wants to stonewall it."

"I can't imagine why," Tom laughed.

"Say's it's just a guy playing dress-up, but I got a feeling. A bad feeling. The way he was described. What he did. How he held his weapon. It doesn't ring true to me that a garden variety psycho would do it like this. They said he was rigid. Almost regimented in the way he attacked."

"So, no *actual* evidence it isn't anyone in a Halloween costume?"

Frank shook his head. "But I think it's kind of beside the point for your purposes, isn't it?"

"How so?"

"Whether on the payroll or not, the public has to be warned. The average joe respects the badge, the uniform. They'll do what a cop tells them. Even walk up a dark alley."

Tom thought for a moment. "Who's he killing? Hustlers? Pushers? Bangers?"

Frank closed his eyes for a few beats before replying. "Just innocent people."

"He sounds like a maniac cop . . ." As he said those words, Tom's eyes lit up. "Maniac cop, that's one hell of a tag."

"Sensationalize it as much as you want," Frank replied, gulping his drink. Make it the biggest story of the year. That's what has to happen before people take notice. If not, more could die. They want people to not know that this asshole dresses as a cop. I think they *have* to know."

"You ready to go on record with this?" Tom asked. "Be quoted directly?"

Frank didn't answer, just stared across the rest of the bar. At all the other cops there, drinking and laughing. None of whom would be happy with him talking to the press.

"Come on," Tom added, also realizing who was around them. "I'll buy you a quart of Jack, and we can go back to my office. Lot more private than this place."

Frank nodded, finishing his glass.

"I'll have to get names and details on the cases," Tom added, standing up and putting his satchel strap over his shoulder. "Can you get me witness names? Medical examiner reports? Etcetera."

"I got all that stuff for you already," Frank said as he threw a twenty-dollar bill on the table. "And I can buy my own whiskey."

As they walked past the throng of officers, who were celebrating being off shift, Frank got to the door and sighed. "Gonna be a lot quieter in here soon enough."

Chapter 3

"It's six o'clock, and now, a news channel exclusive," Tom Shepard began, his voice steady but underscored with a sharp edge. "Tonight, we bring you a story that will, no doubt, send shockwaves through our fair city and one that demands answers from those in charge."

Tom leaned forward slightly, his hands clasped on the desk, his expression grim. "Over the past twenty-four hours, we have learned that the New York Police Department has been withholding crucial information about three recent homicides. And not just any homicides. Witnesses to these brutal murders have described the killer as being dressed as a New York Police Department officer."

He paused for a moment, letting the words sink in, his jaw tightening as he continued. "Think about that for a moment. A symbol of protection, a uniform that's supposed to represent safety and justice, being used as a disguise for murder. Or worse. What if it's not a disguise?"

Tom's gaze locked directly with the camera, his tone growing more personal. "I've been reporting on this city for over twenty years. I've seen its highs and its lows. But this? This shakes me to my core. I've trusted that uniform. We all have. We've taught our children to trust it, to believe that it stands for something truly good. And now, we're left wondering . . . who can we trust?"

He took a breath.

"The victims weren't criminals or gang members. They were ordinary people, going about their lives. A barmaid finishing her shift. A musician heading home. A young couple out for the night. People like you. People like me."

Leaning back, his voice softened. "This isn't just a story for a news cycle. This is a warning. Until the NYPD can guarantee our safety. Until they can tell us the full truth, how can we trust the badge? And why aren't they being honest with us?"

Tom's jaw clenched for a moment before delivering his final blow. "Hiding this crucial evidence from the public effectively means that the blood of the next victim won't just be on the hands of a killer. Commissioner Pike, you owe this city answers. Why have you withheld these salient facts from the public? Why hide that the murderer is either posing as or is, in fact, a police officer of New York City?

And does Mayor Rooke have any clue as to what is going on?"

At his large oak desk in his City Hall office, Mayor Art Rooke listened intently to the News Channel Broadcast. He did not watch the program on the small television but just stared at the newspapers on his desk as he listened to each word.

The broadcast continued . . .

"How can the public protect themselves if they don't know whether a trusted member of New York's police force or someone impersonating one is, in fact, a psychopath with murderous intent rather than their protector? Tune in tomorrow morning for exclusive interviews with witnesses as well as in-depth coverage with Detective Lieutenant Frank McCrae, who is leading this investigation. McCrae, under strict orders not to reveal details about this dubbed Maniac Cop, will provide unique insights into what is a shocking case."

"Goddammit," the mayor seethed, slamming his hand on the desk furiously. "Why can't that son of a bitch Pike control his own men?"

His aide, the perfect lickspittle, who stayed in the periphery until anything was needed and a cheerleader for any of the mayor's inane or misguided requests, slinked forward. "Shall I get McCrae in here for you?"

The mayor scoffed. "Shit, no," he said as he sighed

and rubbed his face with his hands. "Last damn thing I need is someone to think there's a coverup. We can't touch him while this is going on." A sudden thought then came into his head. He pointed to the aide. "I know . . . Draft a statement, that the mayor's office had not been informed about the details of this case or any possible connections between the murders. And that I'm setting up an inquiry board headed by a team of independent experts . . . psychiatrists, psychologists, detectives . . . whatever . . . don't care who . . . just gotta sound good and tick the boxes."

The aide, obediently jotting notes, paused and looked up from his writing pad. "How about we say something nice about the police? I mean about the average cop on the beat. They're the ones that are gonna get the heat for this. Could be good seeing you stand up for them."

The mayor waved dismissively. "That's their shit to handle, not mine."

"And McCrae?"

"Order Pike to let him continue to lead the investigation. If McCrae fails, I'll bust him. If he succeeds, I'll commend him. Then, in six or eight months, when no one remembers this 'maniac cop' bullshit, I'll slice off his balls and eat them in front of him."

Liz Bikoli, thirty-two years old and utterly drained, trudged through the kind of day that felt like the universe had singled her out for cruel and unusual punishment. Clad in worn jeans and a threadbare sweater, she looked as tired as she felt. The relentless storm clouds still loomed overhead, teasing rain and leaving her with a splitting headache for the past twenty-four hours. She had downed more Tylenol than she cared to admit, but it was just enough to dull the pain for her to face the world.

After having been scared about the stories on the news of the Maniac Cop, her first errand of the day was a seemingly simple one, a grocery run. But that spiraled into a cascade of misfortune. As she drove across Fifth Avenue during the pandemonium of the rush hour traffic, her car careened to the side of the street as a tire blew, forcing her to stop half on the curb amid a barrage of honking horns and impatient drivers. Already frazzled, Liz soon wrestled with the jack and spare tire, her frustration mounting as the minutes ticked on by. As she hurried with the last nuts on the tires, she had felt at least some relief. She was so glad no one had stopped to help her. Despite the fact there had been no reports of daytime attacks by the Maniac Cop, she was almost convinced that every car that passed was going to be a police car driven by that monster.

By the time she finally staggered into the grocery store, her hope of salvaging the day quickly evaporated. The items she wanted were most sold out, leaving her with only a small selection of purchases that barely resembled her usual weekly shopping list. She left the store carrying a single paper bag of goods as the weight of this day pressed down on her even harder.

Approaching her car in the fading light of the day, Liz's steps slowed, then stopped as her heart sank. The car door was locked and there, mocking her, were the keys, dangling out of reach as they had been left in the ignition. As she stared, her horror gave way to simmering anger. She stood, one bag of groceries in hand, as the storm clouds above mirrored her mood perfectly.

Leaving her grocery bag by the car, she turned and strode right back into the store, grabbed a pack of clothes hangers from a shelf, and, without even paying for them, walked straight back out into the parking lot.

Within minutes, she was at her car again. The wire from one of the clothes hangers had been stretched out and jammed between the window's glass and rubber seal. As she tried frantically to pick the lock, she had no idea what she was doing but had seen this done count-less times on television. *It couldn't be that hard, could it?* was her only thought.

"Ma'am," a stern voice said from behind. "Hold it right there."

Liz's eyes quickly caught sight in the window's reflection of the young man approaching. She did not see the person. She just saw the uniform and badge.

"Oh shit," she muttered fearfully as her eyes widened.

Hurriedly, she grabbed her handbag that had been slung over her shoulder and rooted around within it.

"Ma'am?" the officer repeated.

Though this was clearly a young police officer, fresh on the job, in Liz's mind, all she could think of was that maniac cop from the news.

Drawing a small pistol from her bag, she turned and aimed it straight at the young officer.

"You're not gonna kill me!" she screamed as she quickly pulled the trigger.

The shot rang out as the bullet smashed through the young officer's glasses, pierced through his eyeball, and burrowed into his brain.

As his body slumped in a heap to the floor, Liz laughed with a nervous relief. Believing she had killed the killer.

Police Captain Ripley sighed. In his sixties, he never thought being a cop would turn into this. Into being shouted at and berated by members of the city council on a daily basis. If you had asked him when he was a recruit what he wanted to be on the force, the last thing he would have said was a paper-pushing punching bag. Yet here he was. Standing in Commissioner Pike's office in front of four angry members of the city council. He would like to think this was a rare occurrence, but it was not. And he put that blame solely at the foot of Pike. But it was not all bad. He only had to wait four more weeks, one short month, and he would be cashing in a retirement check and be far away from all of this.

Pike, meanwhile, was just as annoyed at having to face them. "That woman *thought* he was that maniac, and that gave her license to murder?" He was red-faced and bellowing. "What the hell have we turned into, where we let anyone off after that? She's going down for first-degree murder, simple as that. And her gun? Wasn't even licensed to her. Seems after the damn news report, she took her husband's gun without asking. That's the kind of shit we wanted to avoid by not telling people the details of the case."

"Look," one of the councilmen said, a man who looked too old to be alive, let alone here representing anyone. "We've received several hundred letters of complaints accusing individual police officers—"

"Hold on now," Captain Ripley interrupted, his voice labored and exhausted. "A cop gives anyone a parking ticket these days, of course they're gonna write a letter saying he's a killer. Why? Cos they are assholes, that's why. All the public. Bar none. Assholes. And don't pretend you don't know that."

One of the other councillors, a diminutive woman with a naturally cruel face, took umbrage at Ripley's words as she stepped forward.

"We're all in trouble here, Captain," she shouted. "Tourism over the past few weeks has dropped city-wide. Ever since that damn news report. And you wanna guess how much it dropped by?"

Ripley not only didn't reply, but he was also barely listening to her.

She continued. "Forty-three percent! Forty-three! Theaters and restaurants are down by over half. This is costing us *millions*! We want some damn results. Not just seeing you all here with your thumbs in each other's assholes!"

Pike glanced at Ripley, looking as ever to refocus the blame. "Ripley, if you can't handle this, I'm more than happy to sign off your retirement early. Move McCrae off the case and bring the feds in. We can then get—"

"Not a damn chance," Ripley said, part of him regretting it. But he was never a man to leave anything half-done. "I intend to catch this guy before I leave. McCrae too. Not like we haven't been trying. Yeah, what he did had some bad effects, but the public had a right to know, and we all know that, even if we don't admit it."

"Well, what progress have you made?" the council woman asked pointedly.

"Honestly, at the moment, we're at a loose end. If we stake out Tribeca and Soho, he strikes on the Upper East Side. Like he's one step ahead at each point. We keep changing it around, but we never seem close enough."

The old councilman spoke again, getting as irate as his colleague. "Are you still treating this as if it's not an actual cop? Have you not thought for a *second* that the reason he's one step ahead is that he's got access to all your information?"

Upon hearing it all spelled out in black or white, Pike had no option but to relent. No matter how much he was convinced it was a pretender, he could not deny the facts that, somehow, the killer knew more than he should.

"So, he really *could* be one of our own," Pike said with a grimace.

———

MANIAC COP CLAIMS SEVENTH VICTIM
UNITED NATIONS DELEGATE SLAIN

The headline was bold and needed no more to be said to be understood by every person who happened to see it.

Outside, the evening was settling over Brooklyn as the dark, stormy sky tinged with the faint glow of city lights. Inside a small apartment, the remnants of dinner told their own story. The meatloaf had been cooked, served, and eaten, and the plates were haphazardly stacked in the small sink, waiting for someone to care enough to clean them.

Ellen Forrest sat at the kitchen table, carefully cutting out the headline with a pair of scissors. At twenty-eight, she carried the weight of her life on her shoulders. Married to a cop, her days were a monotonous loop of cooking, cleaning, and occasional brief outings to the salon. The lines of fatigue and sadness etched into her face were impossible to miss. She didn't look like someone who was happy with their life; she looked like someone living on autopilot.

Taking the newspaper cutting, Ellen then stood and walked over to a stack of cookbooks by the oven. Opening one, she placed the cutting alongside the dozen other similar ones already stuffed in between the pages.

In the bedroom, her husband, Jack Forrest, was buttoning up his NYPD blues. Very tall and handsome, he stood in front of the mirror, adjusting his tie with meticulous precision. He caught his reflection and couldn't help but smirk. His vanity was undeniable.

"I didn't know you were working tonight," Ellen said softly as she stepped into the room behind him.

Without looking away from his reflection, Jack replied, "A lot of guys called out sick. The flu's hitting everyone hard, so they need us to cover shifts."

He spoke casually, his tone detached, his focus only on himself.

Ellen sighed, leaning against the doorframe. "It's always at night, Jack. It worries me when you're out so late. Especially with everything."

"Me too, hun," he replied absentmindedly, fastening the buttons on his cuffs, his movements as deliberate as ever.

Ellen walked in and sat on the edge of the bed, watching him with equal parts longing as well as frustration. "You don't talk about your job much anymore." Her voice was tinged with hurt. "It feels like you're shutting me out."

Jack turned to her, a flicker of irritation flashing across his face. "When I come home, I just wanna forget all that. You think I wanna come home and be like . . ." His tone shifted to a mock-happy one. "'Oh, hey, babe, I missed you so much today. Guess what? I just had to arrest a guy after he murdered his four-month-old baby right in front of me. Killed that little sucker with a hammer! I had to carry his little body to the ambulance. What's for dinner?'"

Ellen shook her head, her sadness deepening. "You *used* to want to talk to me."

Jack exhaled sharply, his patience wearing thin. "Hey, you're the one who quit therapy, not me. I was willing to put in the work to fix things. I was the one paying those bills."

"Oh, so it's my fault now?" Ellen shot back.

"I've been doing everything I can to keep this marriage together. And all you do is sit here, acting like the victim. Like I'm the bad guy and you're just putting up with me for all these years."

"You're talking like it's already over," she said as her eyes began to well with tears.

Jack, determined not to let her tears sway the

conversation, shook his head. "It's not enough to just talk, Ellen. You've got to *listen,* too."

"Is that why you're taking all these night shifts? To get away from me? Or is it . . . something else?"

Jack's brows furrowed. "What are you trying to say?"

She hesitated as she took a deep breath. "Jack, sometimes, you wake up in the middle of the night, screaming. Like you can't breathe. And you lash out. I get scared . . . scared you might hurt me or something."

"Where did that come from? I've never laid a finger on you. *Ever!*"

"I know it's wrong to feel this way about my husband but—"

"What the actual hell, Ellen? You've never said anything like this before, not to me, not to anyone. If this was real, why didn't you say something in therapy? Why didn't you say anything *ever*? You can't just blurt that out casually."

Ellen stood and walked toward him, then placed her hands on his chest in a desperate gesture. "Please, Jack. Don't go out tonight. Stay with me. Just this once."

Jack softened slightly as he looked into her distraught eyes. "I can't, Ellen. I'm on the duty roster. I'll make it up to you this weekend, I promise. We'll go to Tarrytown like we used to, okay? Get some fresh air, spend time together?"

As he reached out to pull her into a hug, Ellen stepped back.

"Jack."

"What is it?"

He didn't want to hear the answer, not really. He just wanted to walk out the door, but he was stuck, facing her flitting emotions.

"I don't know what's happening to me. I just don't like being alone in here when you're out all night. I hear things here. I *think* I hear things."

Jack looked confused. What had this argument become? Was it about him still?

"You don't feel safe here? Is that what you're saying? 'Cause we have a gun, and you know how to use it."

Ellen was obviously troubled by the myriad of conflicting thoughts spiraling in her mind and Jack could see this.

"I'll see if I can come back early, okay?" Jack said.

"If I'm asleep, please wake me. Maybe I'm sleeping too much. I read that sleep can cause depression. If that's what this is. Or maybe . . ." Her words trailed off as she just nodded softly to herself and stood from the bed, resigning herself to the situation. "You just go."

Jack didn't know what to do, what had happened. His wife's upset confusing him. What was it really about?

"I'll be home as soon as I can," he said.

As the front door closed, with Jack having left for

the night, Ellen locked the multiple bolts and chains behind him.

As she walked back into the kitchen, she stared at the piles of dirty dishes. *Was this what my life was meant to be?* she thought.

She always had pictured herself as a housewife, but she had always seen children being a big part of that. Jack, though, never wanted them. She knew she compromised too much, but what other choice did she have? She loved him and didn't want to lose him. But was he the man she married?

Deep in thought, she had not even heard the phone when it started to ring. It was only when she stepped forward to run the faucet that she even heard it blaring.

"Hello, Forrest residence?" she said as she picked up the receiver.

There was a beat before a woman's voice spoke over the crackling line.

"He went out again, didn't he?" she said with a tinge of glee.

"What? Who is this?" Ellen suddenly raised her voice at hearing this woman again. "Why do you keep calling me?"

"Why does your Jack keep killing?" The voice almost laughed. "He's gonna do it again, you know?"

The line then cut as the disconnect tone sounded harshly.

Ellen clutched the phone tightly, tears streaming down her face as she wept silently. These calls had become a ritual, arriving like clockwork every time Jack left for his night shifts. Ever since the story of that maniac cop broke, the calls had started.

At first, she'd dismissed them as cruel pranks. Random crank calls preying on everyone's paranoia. But it quickly became apparent this was something else. The caller always knew when Jack had left the house for work, calling within an hour of him shutting the door. And the message was always the same, that *he* was that maniac cop.

The idea was absurd. Impossible. She laughed it off easily. But as the days passed, the notion began to fester in her mind. Jack had been on duty on the nights of each murder. Every time he came home, he seemed more on edge, with a shorter temper, a thinner patience. Was it the stress of the job? Or was there something worse? Was it just their marriage on the rocks? Or had he become a monster?

And then there was the voice on the phone, soft but unsettlingly certain. Who was this woman? Someone in the building who hated her? One of Jack's colleagues? One of his friends? A witness to his crimes? A . . . The thought hitched in her throat every time she considered the other possibility . . . A spurned lover. Or perhaps these calls were not real at all? They could be in her mind. Not like she felt concrete in her own thoughts recently.

With a sudden realization, Ellen bolted across the living room and peered out of the window, down to the street below. There, she caught sight of him, Jack, walking across the street. Lit by the glow of the street-lights, he was on foot, not leaving in his car as he normally would.

Her heart raced. She had to find out.

Whirling, she franticly raced to the closet and pulled on her coat with shaking hands, her mind racing faster than her pulse. She then reached up to the top shelf and grabbed a small shoe box. Opening it, she looked down at the small handgun and box of bullets that lay within.

In his uniform, Jack walked casually down the street. He ignored the many whispered comments of people as they caught sight of his uniform.

"That him?"

"Fuckin' murdering pigs."

"You think that's the Maniac Cop? Fucker looks big enough."

All unoriginal, all laced with either hatred or fear.

Some people didn't even bother to quieten their voices as they walked by.

"Always said the cops were murdering pricks," an eighty-two-year-old woman grumbled loudly as she hobbled by on her walker. A look of disgust on her face aimed at him.

Jack smirked to all of this. Finding it all too

amusing and not caring about the effect his uniform was having on people.

On the other side of the street, having caught up with him, Ellen watched as her husband crossed the intersection ahead, stopping only to avoid the intermittent traffic that ebbed on by. Keeping her distance, she watched his every step from the shadows.

He looked somewhat different to her. He looked bigger. Taller. More confident. She would even go as far as to say that he seemed imposing. Something she would not have guessed he was capable of. But watching him in the wild, she could see that he was not the same man she married. At least he acted differently when he was at home.

Passing a newsstand, her eyes caught sight of various headlines that seemed to scream at her.

MANIAC COP WILL KILL AGAIN

WHO CAN WE TRUST?

MANIAC COP STILL AT LARGE!

The grim words twisted the growing unease in her gut even more.

Averting her gaze from the paper, Ellen caught sight of Jack turning a corner ahead and disappearing from view. Quickening her pace, she soon reached the intersection and slowly peered down the dimly lit street. Lined with neon signs, dive bars, and shadowy after-hours clubs, this was in the opposite direction to the police station, and she knew that all too well.

The knot in her stomach grew even tighter still as she cautiously followed, staying hidden in the shadows as best she could, careful to remain out of sight.

Ahead, Jack walked oblivious to her presence but with purpose. He noticed a pair of grifters standing outside of a club, hurriedly packing away their makeshift Three-card monte game, having caught sight of his approach. If he were on duty, he would have arrested them, but he was not . . . despite what he had told his wife.

Jack then flashed a sly smile at the men as they scrambled to hide their game, their hands fumbling in haste. But he didn't stop as they thought he would. He didn't say a word. He just kept walking, his stride unbroken. The two men froze for a moment before exchanging puzzled glances, their bemusement clear. One shrugged, the other muttered something, but by then, Jack was already fading into the shadows of the street ahead.

Ellen stayed close, her breathing shallow, her nerves shredding. In her mind, she pictured Jack, the man she loved, murdering people. She could not shake that thought. But she also had no idea what she was doing. What would she do if she caught him in the act? She had the gun, but could she bring herself to use it?

Finally, he stopped in front of a three-story motel, with a small parking lot out front. The pink neon sign above the main office's doorway buzzed loudly with an electrical hum as one of the letters flickered on and off erratically. It cast a strange and surreal hue over everything as Jack crossed over the lot, bypassing the office and walked straight over to one of the rooms.

Ellen ducked beside a parked car at the edge of the lot, watching her husband standing at the door to room 3. Her heart raced as she watched him knocking on the door, pausing for a moment, then quietly turning its handle and entering.

Though the curtains to this room were closed, Elle could tell that the light inside had been turned off. As she watched Jack walk into that room and shut the door behind him, that did not change. The room remained in darkness.

A chill ran through her as she edged closer to room 3, moving tightly between the parked cars. A million terrifying possibilities crowded her mind as she silently and nervously padded closer. Each scenario in her head was more horrific than the last.

The line of motel doors were soon in front of her, each one identical save for the room number, and the occasional scuff marks upon it. Quickly reaching room

3, her heart pounded as she pressed her ear to the door, listening for any sound. But she heard nothing.

Her fingers brushed against the door handle. Carefully, she attempted to turn it, but it was locked. Frustrated, she moved over to the window. The curtains were drawn but there, between them was a tiny gap. A crack between the material that could reveal an answer for her.

She leaned in closer, peering into the darkness of the room.

Before she could focus on anything, a hand clamped down on her shoulder, pulling her backward. She almost screamed but managed to catch it in her throat as panic surged through her body. Determined for Jack not to discover her, she stifled all noise.

"Need help, little lady?" the aging motel manager rasped, his voice rough from years of cigarette smoke and cheap whiskey. His milky eyes, dimmed by time but still sharp enough to read people, sized her up. Ellen's neat appearance and composed demeanor stood out in this place, a stark contrast to the parade of hookers, junkies and hustlers he'd watched drift through over the decades. "You lost?"

"I . . . I . . . locked myself out of my room," she stuttered nervously. "Left the key on the sideboard."

"You're staying here?" he asked, taken aback.

Ellen smiled nervously. "Room 3."

"Ah, well, shit happens to the best of us," he said with a chuckle. "It's no problem." He began to root around his pockets for the master key. "You checking out in the morning?"

Ellen could only nod. This man obviously did not know who she was as he was letting her into a room without any demands of identity. Presumably mixing her up with someone else or too embarrassed to say he had no recollection of her. He did remember that a woman had this room, though, and that was enough.

"Be out by eleven, else we charge another day on your bill," he said as he pulled out a set of keys from his pocket and moved over to the door. Quickly unlocking it, the door clicked open quietly.

"Thank you," Ellen replied quietly, not wanting to alert anyone inside of her presence.

The manager nodded to her, then started to walk away. "If ya need me, I'll be at the ice machine. It's been making a racket."

Summoning all her courage, Ellen turned to the opened door. No one had come out to see what was happening or why the door opened. Were they already dead? Had Jack escaped out of the bathroom window? Or was he waiting inside with a knife?

As she stepped onto the threadbare carpet, the glow of the flickering neon sign outside seeped through the door behind her, casting faint, uneven light across the room. It barely broke through the gloom but was enough to reveal the shabby details around her.

This was the living room portion of the suite—if it

could even be called that. The sofa, sagging in the middle and stained beyond recognition, sat at an awkward angle next to a battered coffee table scarred with cigarette burns. An outdated black-and-white TV, its screen dull and dusty, hung precariously on the wall by a loose metal fitting. On the far side of the room, she could see a partially open door. One that led through to another dark room, presumably the bedroom.

Jack was still nowhere to be seen. Had she mixed up the rooms? Did he go in next door?

She briefly considered flicking the light switch on, but her nerves quickly got the better of her. It took every drop of willpower for her to make it across the carpet and head toward the other room.

In the motel parking lot, a truck pulled up. Its headlight beam passed over the room as it drove, casting a quick flash of light inside the still open door, enough to glimpse more soiled details of this dilapidated room.

Getting closer to the room, Ellen blinked hard, attempting to adjust to the darkness in front of her.

Outside, the truck turned again, its lights hitting the room. The flash of light streaked past Ellen and over the crack in the bedroom door for a brief second.

She saw something.

On the chair inside, a police uniform had been tossed haphazardly upon it. Squinting, Ellen soon realized that there were two uniforms on there.

Then a noise.

A deep moan.

One that came from farther inside of the room.

The truck's headlight passed across the room once more as it straightened up in its parking space. The beam came through the front door, across the living room, past Ellen at the bedroom door and over to the bed.

Ellen's heart sank as she saw what it was. Two people under the sheets. Making love.

"No," she whined weakly as she let out a gasp.

"What the hell?" Jack exclaimed, out of breath, as he switched on the bedside lamp.

In his arms, a woman with long blonde hair could not hide her shock at being caught as well as a sudden shame, when she realized who had come into their room.

Ellen could only stare at them, horrified as she tried to form some words.

"You followed me?" Jack gasped.

"I . . . I thought you . . . I thought you were . . ."

Ellen recognized the woman. It was Teresa Mallory. She worked with Jack. Her mind whirred through every time this woman had been mentioned in conversation. Jack nervously falling over her name as he spoke it, while always having some reason as to why she was in the story he was telling. As if he had to justify her being there. Everything had begun to click into place.

"I'm sorry," Teresa said quietly, trying to fight back the tears. "I'm so sorry."

Ellen stared at Jack, looking for answers. Looking for a reason. Hoping in some way this was not what it obviously was. She had come here thinking he was that killer policeman but now . . . Now, she selfishly felt this was much, much worse.

"I didn't want you to find out this way," Jack said, getting out of bed. "I wanted to tell you but didn't know how."

As he walked over to her, Ellen's eyes moved down to his semi-flaccid member. Still sheathed in a condom glistening with moisture.

Ellen felt a sudden rise of sickness in her throat as Jack noticed what she had seen.

"Oh god," he muttered, taking the condom off and grabbing some clothes from the floor. "Let's talk, hun," he said in a panic as she backed away.

"I don't want to hear it," she suddenly shouted as her pain turned to fury. "Don't come near me. Don't ever come near me again!"

Putting on his underwear, Jack stepped nearer to her. "You got every right to hate me. To hate us both. But let me—"

He did not get to finish his pleas before Ellen pulled the revolver from her pocket, aiming it straight at his chest.

"Don't say another fucking word," she shrieked viciously, her hands trembling as she tried to keep her aim steady. "Or I'll shoot you both in your cheating fucking skulls!"

With a cool head, having been at the wrong end of a loaded weapon many times before, Jack raised his hands. Backing away from her, he put himself between the gun and Teresa, who was still in bed, in a flood of silent tears.

"Ellen," he said calmly. "Put that thing down. You don't want to do this."

In shock, Ellen felt her breath getting more ragged, more desperate as the panic took hold. She had to get out of there before she did the unthinkable. Her eyes, full of hate and torment, glared at her cheating husband as her hand still trembled, keeping aim at his chest.

The motel's pink neon sign seemed brighter and more flickery as Ellen rushed out of room 3 and staggered into the parking lot. As she tried to catch her breath, she realized that the gun was still in her trembling grip. Thrusting it back into her pocket, she glanced around, making sure no one had seen her.

"Fuck, fuck!" Jack muttered through gritted teeth, rushing to pull his trousers on.

Teresa, clutching the bedsheet tightly, reached out

and grabbed his arm. "Please, don't go after her. She's not thinking straight. She could shoot you!"

Jack turned, his voice raw with emotion. "Think of how she's gotta be feeling?"

"Nothing we can say or do is going to change any of that." Teresa looked at him with wide, tear-stained eyes. "Maybe in the morning? Maybe you can talk to her then?"

"I gotta go home. I can't stay here tonight," he said with a sigh, not listening to her. "Not now. Not after what I've done."

"What made her even follow you? Did she suspect us?"

"I've got no idea," Jack sighed. "But I'm glad she did. I'm glad it's out in the open. Finally." He took a beat as his guilt weighed down on every thought. "I hated lying to her."

In the parking lot, Ellen came to an abrupt halt as she could not hold back the tears anymore. She stood there and sobbed heavily. It wasn't quiet or restrained; it was a torrent of raw, unfiltered emotion. A guttural moan escaped her lips so profound and heart-wrenching as it echoed around her.

She did not care who heard her. She did not care who saw her.

She was so racked with anguish that she did not see

the car door open a few feet behind her. She was crying too loudly to hear the person getting out of the car and walking toward her.

With her head in her hands, she did not see the large man with extremely broad shoulders getting closer or his NYPD.

As he came to a stop less than a foot away from her and his large boot scuffed on the asphalt beneath, it caught her attention.

Weakly and not really understanding what the noise was, Ellen turned around, expecting to see Jack there. She had no fight in her to scream at him anymore. She hoped that him seeing the pain on her face would say all she needed and that he would just leave her alone.

But it was not Jack.

There was no time to reach for her gun.

One of the terrifying man's arms shot toward her with alarming speed. His gloved hand clamped over her mouth, smothering her scream before it could escape, leaving her gasping for air in silence. His other arm rose. The long, gleaming stiletto knife hovered above her, poised to strike.

In a terrifying blur, the knife sliced down with a brutal precision, its razor blade cutting cleanly across her throat.

She had no idea what had happened, until the hot, wet gush of blood spilled from her wide-opening neck wound, cascading her front and onto the ground, drowning her lungs in seconds.

It was chillingly swift, executed in seconds, leaving no room for resistance or understanding.

The man grabbed her limp, squirming body as the blood choked her. Then, wrenching her backward, he dragged her dying body toward his car. Throwing her into the back seat, she crumpled awkwardly as the blood from her gaping neck wound sprayed arcs of crimson over the upholstery.

Getting into the car after her, he quickly slammed the door behind him.

Across the lot, Jack emerged from room 3, fully dressed in his crisp NYPD uniform. His face was drawn and wearied by what had just happened. Teresa followed close, also in her uniform, complete with a matching expression.

For a moment, they paused under the flickering glow of the motel sign. Without speaking, they embraced, a tender but heavy hug that offered little comfort. Neither of them realized that, something unspeakable had just transpired a few yards away from where they stood.

As they pulled apart, they exchanged a caring, silent glance, before turning and heading off in opposite directions.

Teresa walked in the direction of the precinct,

ready to start her shift, and walked directly past the car where Ellen had been dragged into, oblivious to the horrors still playing out.

Inside that car, Ellen's struggle continued as her final horrific moments were hidden behind the car's tinted windows.

Chapter 4

At 7:53 am, the day arrived on time over the three-story motel. The pink neon sign still flickered over the parking lot, but its glow had little impact as small shafts of sunlight managed to peek through the still heavy storm clouds above.

Sofia Herrera had started in reverse, cleaning the rooms from the top floor of the motel to the bottom. Beginning with room 22, she worked her way back down through the vacant rooms, cleaning them as best she could for the next guests.

As housekeeper for the motel for over a decade, she had cleaned it all. Vomit, semen, blood, you name it; she had wiped up the remnants of it and had to do so as best she could in only a few minutes before moving onto the next room. She knew as well as anyone that this place should have been condemned years ago. The damp, the black mold, the rotten furniture. So, when she cleaned, she could only wipe what was new, not what was already stained and broken. As her mamita told her, *No se puede hacer de un burro un caballo de carrera.* You can't make a racehorse out of a donkey. Sofia preferred *You can't polish a turd.*

"Housekeeping," she called out as she unlocked the door to room 3 with the master key and walked inside. Thankful that the guests seemed to have left already.

With the curtains still drawn, it was a gloomy affair. So, she started the process as she always did.

Curtains open.

Windows open.

All lights on.

Pick up all the trash.

Clean all sideboards and countertops.

Vacuum the living room.

Spray air freshener on everything.

When that was done, she would survey the room for trouble spots. Stains or messes that she could not clean on the cursory sweep of the room.

But there was a smell she could not shake. A stench that seemed to drip off everything. A thick, meaty smell. Rancid and metallic. Putting it down to stale air, she opened the front door as wide as it could so more city air could flow in.

Grabbing fresh towels from the supply cart outside, Sofia then crossed to the door to the bedroom.

In her mind, she ran through her grocery list.

Cleaning on autopilot as she worked out what she needed from the store on the way home.

Sofia believed she had seen it all, yet as she switched on the light, she soon wished she hadn't.

Naked, sitting on the bed and very much dead, was Ellen Forrest.

With her head only connected by a flap of skin at the back of her skull, it hung off her torso at a horrific angle, her eyes upside down to the rest of her, fixed in an open wide stare at the door, at Sofia.

Blood had soaked the entire room. As if it had been sloppily repainted, the red covered every surface she could see.

The humidity in the air made the stink of death so much more pungent. Muck more terrifying.

In the place where Jack and Teresa had made love only hours before, Ellen's corpse had been positioned in the middle of the bed, in a cross-legged seated position. Her hands placed on either side of her. Her body, through the blood, had been pummeled to such a ferocious degree that deep, dark bruises covered her once porcelain skin and stab wounds all over her body.

Sofia screamed so loud that even the manager, fast asleep in the main office, had heard her. People passing on the street had heard her. Everyone in the city was on edge from the news and stormy humidity already that, when anyone heard her screams, they immediately thought of one thing: it was that maniac cop.

.   .   .

An hour later, the bedroom in room 3 had changed. Sofia was gone, having been taken home, and in her place, detectives and a forensic team milled around, looking for clues.

Ellen's body was untouched as a crime scene photographer moved around her, taking as many shots as possible from every conceivable angle.

"Hey, I think I know this woman," one of the detectives said as he turned his head to the side, to better see Ellen's dangling and nearly decapitated head. "She's married to Jack Forrest, right? Helen or somethin'."

Over at the 14th Street Midtown South precinct, Captain Ripley trudged along the stark-white corridor that led to the briefing room. He hated many things about being a cop, but most could be countered with things he loved about the job. He may have hated the hours but loved the unpredictability of the work. No two days were ever the same. He may have hated the bureaucracy, but he thrived on the camaraderie of the people here, a motley crew who, for all their flaws, had each other's backs when it really mattered. At least they did before this killer appeared. Now, though, was the part of the job he hated the most. The one thing that could not be countered. There was nothing redeemable about what he had to do now, aside from the fact that someone *had* to do it. And being the captain, he saw it as his responsibility.

He pushed open the door to the briefing room. The murmur of chatter and the scrape of chairs greeted him as he interrupted the morning assignments.

The detective leading the briefing looked up from his paper. "Captain? All okay?"

Ripley walked in and looked around at the two dozen uniformed officers sitting there. "Can I borrow Forrest for a moment?"

Jack Forrest sat at the back, peered at the captain with a look of confusion. "What did I do now?" he asked playfully.

Ripley did not answer, just smiled politely and motioned to the door beside him.

"Guess the cap heard how awesome I am!" Jack joked as he stood. "It's on to bigger and better things."

Ripley led the way out of the room and down the corridor, his expression laced with dread.

Jack followed closely, making small talk. "Hey, Cap, you decided where you'll settle down to retire yet? I knew some folks who went to Sarasota. They say it's the place to be."

With no reply, Ripley stopped at a door to a small office, opening it.

"Cap, what is this?" Jack asked with a sudden look of concern. "This not a reassignment? Thought we were going to another station or something."

•　•　•

As they sat at the small table in the vacant office, Jack looked increasingly worried at what this could be about. Did he not log all the drugs he busted? Did he take evidence home by mistake? Did he roughhouse a suspect? He had no idea. He was a clean cop, as far as he was aware. Sure, others may have found him a slight bit narcissistic and a prick at times, but that wasn't an offense . . . Was it?

"Jack," Ripley said in a maudlin tone. "It's about your wife."

Rolling his eyes, Jack couldn't hide the smirk. "Lemme guess, she called you? Complained about me?"

"Excuse me?"

"I thought she would have called a lawyer, not my job." Jack sighed loudly. "I'm so sorry, Cap. This won't affect anything here. It's just not working out. Ellen and me. We're gonna file for divorce soon."

Ripley regarded Jack with curiosity for a moment. "So, you haven't been getting along?"

"I'm sorry?" Jack asked, suddenly realizing where he was and who this was. "But, with all due respect, what business is it of the NYPD's if I'm having trouble in my marriage?"

"Jack, I'm sorry. There is no easy way to tell you any of this." Ripley closed his eyes for a second, considering the best words. "We got a call at about 8 a.m. Your wife's body was found."

Jack's expression fell. "She's . . . what? Dead?"

Ripley nodded. "And it does not seem to be an accident or self-inflicted—"

"*What?*"

"So, your marriage and how it was *is* NYPD business, as we have to open an investigation."

"How did she die?" Jack asked, barely even audibly.

"Do you really want to know the details?"

Jack did, one hundred percent, not want to know the grisly details. He *needed* to know them.

"Just say it."

"Okay . . . She was discovered by the cleaning lady in a sleazy motel off Eleventh Avenue. She was naked and had her head almost cut off."

"You gotta be wrong. You're wrong. It's a joke, right?" Jack let out a nervous chuckle. "You fucking with me? Did Ellen put you up to this as revenge?"

"This is not a joke," Ripley said in all seriousness.

"But she ran out of the motel." Jack's thoughts whirled. "I thought she went back home!"

"Ran out? You were there?"

"I tried to stop her, to talk sense, but she had a gun. She pointed a gun in my face."

This was not how Captain Ripley envisioned this meeting to go. Of course, all partners should be considered as primary suspects in any murder case's inception, but it was still rare to be the answer. Though, as Jack spoke, he had proven three things to Ripley.

Jack Forrest was having trouble in his marriage, his

wife had confronted him with a weapon, and he confirmed his presence at the location of the crime.

The three red flags suddenly changed what was a delivery of bad news to the start of a new line of inquiry.

"Office Forrest," Ripley said matter-of-factly. "Before you say anything more, I better read you your rights."

The morning had turned into the evening as Jack sat in a small holding cell. Out of his uniform and dressed in jogging pants and a T-shirt given to him by the booking sergeant, he had been remanded on suspicion of being involved in the murder of his wife. He was placed in a separate cell from where the usual criminals were held and, instead, was in what they called a protected services cell. One reserved for criminals who needed protecting or celebrities or emergency services workers under suspicion.

When they told him of Ellen's death, Jack knew what was about to unfold. Unsurprisingly, they held him, and he did not kick up any fuss. It was all part of the job, and Jack knew that, when they had concluded their investigation, he would be released. He just had to sit through this and wait.

Even when they notified him of their search of his and Ellen's apartment, he nodded without saying a word. What would they find? A few dirty magazines shoved under a loose floorboard? Ellen's vibrator?

Ellen.

Damn.

Every time he thought of her, he did so in the present tense. As if she was at home waiting. Not . . . not murdered.

In the silence of his cell, he cried for hours. Despite all he had done to ruin their marriage, he loved her. He still loved her.

As the evening began, Jack was moved from his holding cell and into a stark, windowless interrogation room. He looked pale and in shock as he rested his wrists heavily on the cold metal table in front of him. He was at a loss of words, and his eyes were bloodshot from crying. To his right, a tape recorder whirred loudly, a mechanical hum as the reels of tape spun, capturing every second of this interview.

Across the table, Captain Ripley sat next to the lead investigator Frank McCrae, who was looking exhausted after spending the previous night on another stakeout. One that proved to be yet another dead end.

"We found these in a cookery book in your apartment," Frank said as she opened a folder in front of Jack and pulled out a handful of press clippings.

Staring down at them, Jack looked at each headline in confusion. All were about that maniac cop.

"What is this? These ain't mine."

Frank nodded as he pulled out a small book. One that Jack recognized: Ellen's diary. Frank opened the diary to a bookmarked page and began to read. "Thursday. I got another call. They keep saying Frank's that killer. That killer cop from the news. I don't want to believe it. I really don't."

Jack stared, aghast.

"Is that why she followed you?" Ripley asked. "Is that why she was murdered? Because she found out your little secret?"

Frank didn't wait for Jack to answer before adding in his own question. "Do you have an alibi for last Wednesday night? Or the preceding Friday?"

"I . . . I was home."

Ripley shook his head. "If you were home, your wife wouldn't have suspected you now, would she?"

Jack did not know why he just lied about where he was. It was not like any of this could remain a secret much longer, not if he wanted to ever be released. "Okay, I was . . . seeing someone. It's *why* Ellen was angry at me. Not 'cause of any of this shit about being a murderer."

"Why did you just lie about where you were?" Frank asked.

"I *don't know*! Okay? I'm used to lying about it to Ellen. I . . ."

The door to the room opened, and a pudgy, sweaty

man walked in, complete with an angry look. Raymond Jessop, Public Defender.

"This is over," he bellowed. "I'll talk to my client alone now, please."

Ripley turned to the lawyer. "We read him his Miranda rights," he said with annoyance. "And he's elected to make a statement voluntarily."

Jessop waved his hand as he walked around the table. "It's inadmissible, and you know full well of that. He is required to get legal counsel before any interrogations. No matter what."

Frank kept quiet. He knew full well of the laws that protected civil liberties, and he was against most of them as he had seen them twisted on countless occasions leading to a guilty person walking free.

Ripley, though, was not going to keep his mouth shut. "He's acknowledged he was in the motel room. He admitted his wife pointed a gun at him—"

"Now, now, Captain." Jessop shook his head in disapproval. "You know none of that can be used. After he gets council, if he says that, then you can use it. Otherwise, you got bubkes. Get out of here."

Frank stood, picking up the press clippings and putting them back in the file. "Come on, Captain. We'll pick this up later."

When they had left and the tape recorder had been switched off, Jessop pulled up a chair next to Jack. "How you holding up?"

"As good as can be expected." Jack shrugged. "They're making me the fall guy for this, aren't they?"

Jessop nodded. "But I'm certain you had no control over what you did. Call it an irresistible impulse. That's a legal defense we can use for this. Or better yet, maybe you don't even remember committing the crimes. Blackouts. Momentary lapses of memory. Stress from the job. Stress from home. Stress—"

"Wait," Jack said. "I didn't do this, and I'm not crazy."

"Well, you *were* seeing a therapist, and that works in your favor."

Jack let out a groan of annoyance. "A fucking *marriage* counselor. Not a damn therapist."

Jessop did not react to this outburst. He had seen this behavior time and time again with his clients. They all pleaded innocence. Even if caught with the murder weapon in their hands. And he saw this man, this cop, as being no different from any other accused criminal. He wasn't paid enough by the Legal Aid Society to care, so he just fought for his clients as best he could and left it all at the door when his day ended. He did not fight the good fight; he just fought for a paycheck.

"Look," Jack said. "I've got a witness. Okay?"

Jessop's interest was suddenly piqued.

"Oh, you do?"

"Someone else who was there last night. In the

motel. I didn't want to bring her into this unless there's no other way."

Jessop chuckled. "Brother, you need all the help you can get. You've seen how much they're baying for blood. They think you are guilty, with only loose circumstantial evidence. If you have a witness, you get them on your side now. Nip this in the bud as soon as possible."

"But this could ruin her career if it all goes south." Jack then pondered on this for a second. "Let's give it till the end of the week. If they don't find the real killer by then, I'll name her."

The television screen in Jake's Saloon flickered with grainy images of New York City streets as Tom Shepherd, the news anchorman, delivered his introduction to a new special news report. "The city that never sleeps remains under siege, gripped by the terror of the Maniac Cop, who still remains at large." He spoke in a low, measured tone. "With the possibility of this being one of the very figures sworn to protect them, the residents of New York are, understandably, still very angry and confused. Don't believe me? Listen to them for yourselves."

The report cut to the series of vox pops, speaking in hurried, raw interviews.

The first was a woman in her forties, out on the

streets. "I gotta tell my kids . . . You see a cop, you run like hell. You cross the street, you don't stop for no one. And that's not right!"

Her voice shook as the camera moved to show her clutching her young daughter's hand.

The report then cut to a young man sitting on a stoop and shaking his head. "I've seen friends of mine murdered by cops. Shot in the back. Shot when they got no gun, no knife, no nothin'!" His voice quickly rose with frustration. "Why people acting like this is new? Cops like killing folks, that's why they're cops!"

Next, a teenager with a mop of long hair leaned against a graffitied wall. His eyes were bleary in a marijuana haze, and he smiled goofily. "Cops want you to be scared of them, right?" he said. "Who's to say this isn't a fix-up job run by the government to keep us in line?"

Next, an older man, weathered and weak, sat on a park bench. "We respected the police back in my day. The blues and badge meant something. If you stepped out of line, they busted your head. They didn't take no guff. They were the law. But still, they protected ya. Nowadays, kids have no idea."

His gravelly voice faded as a stern-looking woman, arms crossed and standing by a bus stop, spoke directly to the camera, not the interviewer. "It took this crazy SOB killin' folks to cut crime?" she said. "Before you had kids out muggin' and rapin', now with *him* out there, nobody wants to be out on the streets when they don't have to. So, maybe it's not all bad!"

The report then moved to silent footage of a nearly empty street at night, where only a lone police squad car slowly cruised past the camera.

Tom Shepherd's narration returned, heavy with foreboding. "As fear spreads through the streets and trust in law enforcement crumbles, New Yorkers are left to wonder . . . Who can you call when the badge becomes the threat?"

At his regular booth in the Saloon, Frank McCrae had ignored the news report and just talked with Captain Ripley, who sat opposite him. Both men had a whiskey and looked beyond exhausted. They were in the middle of trying to work through the case.

"I get what you're saying," Frank said. "But this asshole doesn't murder his wife. He butchers strangers. I don't see the correlation between Forrest and the Maniac Cop."

Ripley leaned in. "We had a real bizarre case once, about eighteen or nineteen years ago. Women were winding up dead. Each of them shot in both eyes. We naturally linked them to one serial killer. Then we got damn lucky and caught a break in the case. We found a fingerprint at one of the crime scenes. It turned out it was the son of one of the previous victims. This guy killed seven people in all and put his mom in the middle of them, just to make sure no one looked to him as the killer. Thinking he was just a victim's relative. One among many. We were lucky he was dumb enough to leave a print, or he would have gotten away with it." He smirked. "People do the stupidest, most insane stuff. And in this case, it's as strong scenario as any. It's possible at least. So, we gotta look at him as if he is our guy."

"I get what you're saying, but I think it's the opposite. I think Jack Forrest was set up to take the heat off the real killer," Frank said. "I've met him a few times on the beat. Nice enough kid. Dumb as a brick, and I can't see him having the brains to do what this maniac cop guy has done. And the killer positioned the body for us to see. The others were just as they fell. So, this was a statement."

"You really think this killer's *that* smart?"

"Damn right, he is." Frank took a swig of his whiskey. "He's smart enough to kill with no real witnesses, no evidence left. Look at all the killers you've seen before. Most don't make it past two kills. They leave something behind, witnesses that can identify them."

"But he left that woman in the car, after he killed her boyfriend."

Frank smirked. "And could she identify a thing about him aside from his size and what he wore?"

"And you still think he's a real cop?"

"I got no doubt in my mind. This guy knows procedures and has evaded us so far. I can't see John Q Public being able to do that."

"Come on!" Ripley protested.

"Either way, if there really *is* a witness, like Forrest's lawyer claims, his name will be cleared, and we are back to square one. I think we need to look inward at the NYPD."

"You know this witness of Forrest's? It could just be a distraction."

"Sure." Frank shrugged. "But if they do exist and Forrest is keeping their identity secret, I'd bet my last nickel the killer also knows who they are, too. And if that witness has anything that can blow this frame job —that's if my hunch is correct—then Frank and them are definitely in danger."

"So, what do we do? We got zero to go on. It's all your guessing."

"Only one thing we can do," Frank said as he finished his drink and stood up from the booth. "We gotta get Forrest to talk."

"That's a load of bull," Jack exclaimed in annoyance, pacing in the protected holding cell. "How is me keeping quiet putting her in danger? Huh?"

Frank, perched on the corner of the bed, found it hard to contain his satisfaction at what was just said. "So, your witness is a woman?" he remarked. "Presumably, a woman you were having an affair with? Your wife caught you in the middle of it, I guess? Hence the gun? Makes sense."

Jack glared at Frank.

"I'm not meaning to piss you off here, but wives don't go off the deep end and point a weapon unless they found out their husband was off and getting their dicks wet with someone else."

"You know damn well that if I give you a name, you could railroad her just like you railroaded me!"

Jack's annoyance was evident and understandable, at least to Frank.

"This killer, this maniac cop, or whatever he's called . . . I think he set you up, wanted to frame you."

"Frame? Me?"

Frank got up from the bed to meet Jack on his level. "Look at your story. You—and I'm presuming this mystery woman—were in bed. Ellen then walked in. Caught you. She pointed the gun at you. Got angry, then left. You and the mystery woman leave the motel soon after. This guy must have seen all that and decided to murder your wife, then waited for you to leave. When the coast was clear, he broke into the room without breaking the lock and positioned your wife's body. And all that is too much effort to not be exact and deliberate."

"But why me? Why pick me? What have I done?"

Frank shrugged. "Could be anything. Your size. How you look. He could have dark hair and is big as you. Or could be revenge for something you've done in some interaction with them on the job—*if* they're a cop, that is. Reasons aside, they have all the information on you. And knew you were already having an affair and who it was with. Wasn't sure of the moment. I think he probably also had help."

"Ellen's phone calls?"

Frank nodded. "Ellen's diary detailed how they happened every time you left the house for work. So, whoever it was calling was also watching you. Planning it. I wonder how many times the killer followed you when a call was made and they hoped Ellen followed you?"

"But nobody knew," Jack said, unable to fathom how this all clicked together.

"If you didn't tell anyone? And no one ever saw you, then this woman you're protecting sure as hell told someone." Frank's words were sincere. "So, she *needs* to be protected, and I can protect her."

"She can take care of herself. She outshoots me every time we go to the range."

Thinking for a moment, he soon realized that Frank McCrae was indeed right. She could be in danger from this monster as well as hold the key to who it was and who the woman on the phone to Ellen was. He had no option but to name her. If he didn't, something awful could happen.

"Teresa Mallory."

"Mallory? Really? On your squad." Frank looked shocked as Jack sheepishly nodded. "Well, congratulations, I had no idea." Frank pursed his lips. "You know? There is another possibility."

"What?"

"Aside from the fact it could just be a crank and unrelated to the murders, the person leaving those calls could be Mallory. You know that, right?"

Jack didn't want to admit that to himself or this detective, but he knew it was true. The diary excerpts he had been read during the interrogations were quite clear. Someone, some woman, had been tormenting Ellen with this lie. The lie that he was to blame. He then had a thought he hated to consider.

"Do you think she could have had anything to do with this? She might be in league with the Maniac Cop?"

Frank regarded Jack with surprise. "Of course, it's possible, just as you being the killer is *possible*. This guy could also just as easily be a few people, not just one. We know the description of the large white male in a uniform. There could be much more behind it. Everything I am saying here is all supposition. That is detective work. You make a guess, check it out. If it's wrong, look at the evidence and make another guess." Noticing Jack's demeanor turn sadder with confusion, Frank changed tack. "But anything is possible. So, don't think bad of her quite yet."

Jack wiped the sweat from his brow. "You know what's funny? Ellen loved murder mysteries. She would have loved to have heard all these bits of information. She could have cracked the case wide open." Jack closed his eyes, stuck on the painful memory of what he had done. "She would be alive if I had kept it in my pants, wouldn't she?"

Frank agreed but didn't reply. There was no point kicking this man when he was already down.

Chapter 5

Tonight wasn't a night when normal pedestrians roamed freely. The sidewalks had become eerily sparse, aside from the usual parade of criminals and sex workers who could not let the thought of any "maniac cop" deter them from plying their trade. No murderer on the prowl would stop flesh and drugs from being sold to the fastest bidder. Instead, the buyers had taken to the streets, which bustled with cars as they slowed down to survey what was on offer, like a roadside buffet.

Out of the shadows and into a streetlamp's light, a woman stepped forward with a deliberate, confident sway. Her wardrobe was provocative, perfectly suited to the role: a tiny leather skirt clinging precariously to her hips, leaving little to the imagination, while a strapless Lycra top accentuated her chest. She blended seamlessly into the world in which she infiltrated, and to the untrained eye, she was just another working girl standing on the block, selling her sex for cash.

But this wasn't just any hooker. Beneath the teased hair and layers of makeup, Officer Teresa Mallory was barely recognizable in her undercover role.

Her heart quietly raced as she stepped down the street, scanning her surroundings as she inhabited her new character.

A honk of a car horn grabbed her attention. When she turned, Teresa saw an old, piggy-looking man sat behind the wheel of his car, wearing thick milk bottle glasses.

"How ya doing, beautiful," he called out, with a genuine look of happiness as he pulled over to the curb.

"How am I doing? That depends, handsome," she replied with a playful smirk, stepping to the open passenger window.

"You busy?" he asked.

Teresa looked around, before leaning on the open window. "Now do I look busy to you?"

"Haven't seen you 'round here before." He sniffled as he pushed his very thick glasses up the bridge of his nose. "I know all the girls, but you're new, right?"

"Maybe you haven't looked hard enough? I've been about."

He smiled and motioned to the empty passenger seat. "How about a lift somewhere?"

"A lift?" she said, biting her lip seductively. "I'm at home here. I don't need a lift."

"Could I interest you in something else, then?" the man asked with growing trepidation.

For him, this seemed more difficult than usual. The girls would say yes to a lift. 'Lift' being a code word.

"Want to be a little more specific?" Teresa asked. "What is it you really want?"

The man's smile dropped. "Hey, you wouldn't be a cop, would you? You gotta tell me if you are, you know?"

Teresa blew her cheeks out in annoyance. "You asked the jackpot question. Now you get to go home and kiss your grandkids with that dirty mouth."

Slowly turning back to the street, the driver nodded. "I'll be going, then?"

"Yeah, you do that."

"But I'll be thinking of you the whole time," he added cheekily as his car pulled away and sped off down the street.

"Can't arrest you for that," Teresa muttered. "Ya damn weirdo."

As she stepped back onto the sidewalk, she breathed a sigh of relief. That guy was too old and tired to make it in any prison, so she was glad he made her as a cop before any arrest.

This was one of the parts of the job she had to disassociate herself from. She saw no problems in a woman selling her body if they chose to. If they were not being pressured to do so, or for any nefarious reason, then to her, it was a totally fine profession. But she was a cop. It was her job to think otherwise. She was not there to enforce only the laws she agreed with, but she had to do what was asked, which she did with aplomb. Working vice and despite her disagreements with the laws, she had found herself damn good at ensnaring the johns on the days she was undercover. And every single time she did it, she always found one common thread between them: they were married and with kids.

"Maybe we'll get the next one," she said in a hushed tone.

But she was not talking to herself. Concealed along the lining of her top, taped to her collar bone, was a wire. One that heard everything she said. A monitor for any backup. But this was only a one-way conversation. An earpiece would have been too obvious on these streets, so a block away, parked in an unmarked sedan, was her partner, an officer called Malone. He only had one job: to wait out of sight and collect any arrests.

Glancing at her wristwatch, she noted the time before looking toward both ends of the street. The other sex workers who were here avoided eye contact as they always did. An agreement between them and the cops ensured Teresa could operate without any interference. And in exchange, the law would turn a blind eye to these real workers who would continue to be allowed to ply their trade without fear of arrest. But when they looked away, it stung Teresa. She knew they saw her as the enemy.

Over the next hour, the steady flow of cars had begun to dwindle, till there was no business left for anyone. Tonight was done. There was no more johns, and one by one, the other women here, as well as the hustlers and the dealers who worked the shadows, all called it a night and headed for their homes.

Teresa was the last person on this street, as she finally gave up as well. With no arrests, it had been her least successful night in vice ever.

"I'm calling it, okay?" she spoke under her breath into the wire. "No point staying out longer."

She reached into her clutch handbag, which only had space to carry four things, her small police-issue gun, her badge, a pack of cigarettes, and a lighter. A couple of moments later, she was inhaling her first smoke of the night. It was her little reward to herself, having recently given up a pack a day. She had made the mental pact to only smoke when she finished a night shift or had sex. And that night's couldn't have come quick enough. This night had dragged so slow. All waiting and no action.

Peering either way down the street, there was no sign of Malone. Usually, he would have pulled the car around when she finished and driven her back to the station.

"Dammit," she grumbled as she decided to walk.

She could not wait around any longer. Knowing

Malone, he had seen everyone leaving and gone himself, without even coming to get her. At least she lived nearby. Not like she had to traipse all the way to the precinct dressed like this. Only a few blocks.

Turning a corner as she took a long drag from her cigarette, a shadow crossed in front of her.

She stopped in her tracks and looked up.

Nothing was there.

Nothing but a sound.

She could hear footsteps. The heavy clacking of boots, fast approaching from somewhere but not from a particular direction. On these dark, vacant streets, the sound reverberated down the brick buildings around her.

"Hello?" she called out. "Malone? That you?"

The footsteps continued to get closer. Louder.

"Malone?" she said again.

Turning, she then saw where the footsteps came from. Someone was coming toward her from the shadowy street behind her at a slow pace. From his gait and size, she could tell it wasn't Malone, but it was a cop.

She quickly reached for her handbag and brought out her badge. She knew that any cop would arrest her for the way she was dressed, rightly assuming she was out to solicit sex. She held it up toward him before she could even see his face. "Officer Mallory, Fourteenth Precinct. Vice Squad."

This figure gave no reply. He just continued

walking toward her slowly. In his hand, she could clearly see a billy club, and with each step, he twirled it expertly around his wrist. Attached by the strap, he spun it, then caught it again in his palm. Something she hadn't seen since her dad was on the force. A beat-cop maneuver they all used to do with their clubs.

Releasing the club, he spun it around his wrist again, catching it on its return. Then back around again. The deep thumping sound it made as his white gloves caught it beat in time with his step.

Getting about ten feet away, Teresa quickly realized who this figure was.

The figure then suddenly stopped in his tracks as he caught his billy club again, spun it around in his grip, and twisted the handle off, quickly pulling it apart to reveal the long, savage-looking, stiletto knife he had used on many occasions. On many kills.

Without breaking her stare at the man, backlit by the streetlight behind him, her hand rushed into her clutch and immediately withdrew her revolver.

"Malone?" she said aloud with urgency as she spoke into her wire. "Ten-thirteen. Officer needs assistance." She kept her aim on the cop as she backed away slowly "I need backup. It's the Maniac Cop. Get your ass over here *now*."

With each step she took back, the gigantic figure then advanced a step as if playing a game.

His eight-point cap cast his face into darkness, but the blade of the knife shone as he held it out.

"Ten-thirteen. Officer needs assistance."

She stepped back. The figure stepped closer, his stride much longer than hers.

"Ten-thirteen, Malone? *Anyone?* He's here! It *is* a cop!"

Closer.

Gritting her teeth, she finally stopped and put both hands on her gun. "Police!" she said loud and clear. "One more step, and I'll blow your damn brains out."

Frank sped through the shadowy streets of the city, his eyes darting to every figure that passed him on the sidewalk. He scrutinized each one, searching for Teresa Mallory. But she wasn't among them. The ones who met his gaze responded with teasing winks or by blowing a kiss, oblivious to his actual intent.

He had only just learned she'd been assigned to the streets that night, and that thought tightened in his chest. Every bone in his body told him that she was the next in line for the maniac lurking in the city. Frank knew he had to find her before it was too late.

Frank's tires screeched as he pulled his car to the curb. He threw it into park and leaped out, rushing toward the alley where Officer Davis Malone was supposed to be stationed. The backup for Teresa.

Two sharp cracks of gunshots then split the air from a few streets away, freezing Frank mid-step. For a heartbeat, he, as well as the city, held its breath.

After the sound dissipated, he rushed farther into the alley, immediately seeing the dark sedan parked up, with somebody sat behind the wheel.

"Officer Malone!" he shouted as he rushed to the car. "Have you got contact with Mallory?"

As he pulled open the door, the body of Davis Malone slumped out onto the dirt. A large gash on the side of his head, he was still alive but had been knocked unconscious, then placed back into his car.

Then came a third shot.

Damn, Frank thought as he took off in a dead run of the alley. Before setting off in the direction the shots had come from, he raced over to his car, yanked open the door, and grabbed the radio.

"This is Detective Frank McCrae. Backup needed. I repeat, backup needed. East of Homburg Street. Send units *now*!"

He had no time for propriety. No time to give his badge number or wait for a reply. He just needed more officers on the scene.

Pulling his gun, he took off down the street on foot.

"Officer Mallory!" he shouted as his voice and sound of his running cut through the otherwise silence. "Officer Mallory!" he called again, louder, more desperate.

Up ahead, he soon noticed a section of the street where the streetlights had been knocked out, casting it into a deep darkness. The glass from them scattered over the shadowy ground.

Feeling a creeping dread, he slowed his pace. As he did, his boots crunched softly on slivers of broken shards beneath him. His breaths came in shallow puffs as he gripped his gun, leveling it in front of him, ready to fire at the first sign of trouble.

Before his eyes could adjust to see what lay in the black recesses around him, a weight slammed into his side, knocking him backward and down onto the sidewalk. His back slammed into the glass fragments as his pained gasp mixed with someone else's scream, Teresa's . . . as she landed on top of him like a sack of potatoes.

The Maniac Cop did not spare a second. He stepped out of the shadows like an approaching freight train and grabbed Teresa by the back of her neck. With an almost impossible strength, he hoisted her into the air, cutting her scream short, then slammed her back down onto Frank with tremendous force.

The impact knocked the breath out of Frank and knocked his gun from his grasp. Dazed, he barely registered Teresa's limp body sliding off him as an intense pain flared through his chest. He tried to focus, but there was no time as the hulking brute stood above him.

Frank raised one arm instinctively to shield himself as his other hand frantically swept the ground beside him, searching for his fallen weapon.

The blade of the stiletto knife quickly slashed downward, slicing through the flesh of Frank's palm.

As he cried out in pain, the fingers on his other hand touched cold steel. Gritting his teeth against the pain, Frank curled his fingers around the gun he just found.

BANG.

The first shot hit the figure point-blank in the chest.

BANG.

BANG.

BANG.

Each bullet was a kill shot to the heart.

But the huge shape did not fall.

Instead, he raised the stiletto knife in the air once again and towered above Frank.

From down the street, a group of flashing lights suddenly appeared with sirens blaring out as three police vehicles sped toward them.

Teresa lifted her eyes, barely holding onto consciousness as the cars pulled up, and the armed officers rushed out toward them.

"Freeze, hold it right there!" they shouted.

But as they arrived, guns drawn, the Maniac Cop was gone. Frank was left staring up in shock, his gun still aimed up to where the figure was.

"Put the gun down," came the call from the policemen.

"We're cops," Frank replied, dropping his arm, grabbing the badge from his belt with his bloodied hand and lifting it up high. "Detective Lieutenant

Frank McCraw. This is Officer Mallory, undercover vice."

"We got calls for backup? That you?"

As both were helped to their feet, Frank ignored the pain in his hand and the new soreness of his cracked ribs.

"Where did he go?" Teresa asked, her voice pained and sore as she gripped onto the officer's jacket for balance.

"I hit him. I swear I did," Frank muttered in shocked confusion. "I hit him dead in the chest. Right through the heart."

"I pumped two into his head," Teresa added as she tried to put weight on her ankle, but it was too sore.

"*Who* were you shooting at?" an officer asked.

"It was him, the Maniac Cop . . . but . . ." Frank shrugged. "He didn't go down."

As Frank helped Teresa back to his car, the officers swept the scene for any trace of the killer.

"D'you see his face?" Frank asked. "Can you identify him?"

She shook her head. "I was too busy trying to stay alive."

Back in the safety of Jake's Saloon, Frank felt that familiar numbing as he downed his third glass. He needed to dull the pain that radiated from his bandaged hand and ribs and had been quite successful in this attempt.

"Back again?" the barman had asked as he and Teresa walked in an hour before closing.

With the bar winding down after the raucous crowds had left, it only left the hardened drinkers or those with nowhere else to go.

Now sat in his familiar booth at the rear of the bar, Frank wrestled with what he and Teresa were discussing.

Dressed in her normal attire, Teresa sipped a beer. Each swallow she took was sore, her throat bruised from her attacker's terrifying grip.

"His hands were huge," Frank said, pointing to the bruising around her neck.

Teresa was still in shock but doing her best to mask it. "Even through the gloves, he felt like ice," she said, her voice hoarse. "And he held me right up against his chest. It was all like an ice block. I couldn't even feel him breathing. When I shot him, he didn't make even a sound."

"We better leave that out of the report," Frank replied.

He had heard her say this a few times. That the man was cold. Not breathing. After shooting him a few times and him not falling, Frank could not say for a fact that she was mistaken. But he did not believe her either. How could he? She was saying he was like a walking corpse.

"Why did you come looking for me? Malone said he didn't have time to call it in before he was attacked."

"You're Jack's only witness. If I was right and this cop was behind the murder of his wife and trying to set him up, it then stands to reason that he would have to come after you. That's why he simply didn't carve you up and leave you behind. He grabbed you, right? As if he was wanting to take you with him. He didn't want to leave another body before Jack was sent down for his crimes." Frank picked up his nearly empty drink. "That's my theory anyway." He sank the last few drops.

"That's why Malone was only knocked out. To hide the connection to the other killings?"

"It's just a theory, but it connects all those dots. I just don't know why, though. What's the end game. So, he sets Jack up. They blame him. Then what? He stops?"

Teresa had been told about Ellen's demise and Jack's arrest on the ride back to the station. She could not believe any of it. She confirmed with Frank that she was with Jack that night and backed up his story verbatim. As she sat here, she felt like she needed to cry, scream, and shout. But could not find the ability to do any of it.

"This guy may be a 'maniac,' but he's far from dumb," Frank said as he motioned to the bartender for another round of drinks.

"What do we do now?" Teresa asked with a small

cough. "If I'm in danger, do I go into protective custody? Do I go back to mine?"

"Oh, hell no," Frank grimaced. "This guy seems to know the ins and outs of what we do. We can't trust any police procedures at all. If he knew where you were tonight, which was not publicly announced, then we can take it as read that he knows where you live."

The bartender silently arrived with a new beer and triple shot of whiskey. Placing them on the table, he left with a nod to Frank.

"The plan is," Frank continued, "we have one more drink, then I'm taking you home with me. I've got a nice foldout couch you can crash on."

He may have seemed accommodating and careful, but Frank knew exactly what he was doing. He knew that, somehow, she was more linked to this case than she let on or knew. After she had been attacked, his theory that she could be in on it was put to rest but as for the question of who harassed Ellen with those phone calls . . . that was another matter.

"I meant to ask," Frank said, sneaking his intended questions among the other talk. "Who did you tell about the affair?"

"Excuse me?"

"I'm not meaning to pry, but this guy knew about you and Jack and the motel and not by happenstance."

Teresa looked confused. "I guess I told my sister about it on the phone."

"Your sister?"

"But she lives in Cincinnati."

"Oh." Frank thought for a moment, making it seem as if he hadn't planned every question in his mind already. "Anyone on your team know?"

"Why the hell would I do something dumb like that?" Teresa took a sip of her beer as the newer pint lay in wait at the edge of the table. "If I let on with them, I may as well kiss my chances of promotion away."

"I think that's a bit far-fetched."

Teresa shook her head. "For a female officer to break up another officer's marriage in New York of all places? It may be legal to do, but the cops here would put a fucking scarlet letter on me."

"No one? You *definitely* told no one?"

"Nobody that could have been involved."

"So, there *is* someone else?"

Before she could answer, in order to gauge her reactions, he added, "Jack was deliberately set up, you know that. But what I didn't tell you was that somebody got his wife to follow him. She'd been getting prank calls from a woman. Now as I see it, he didn't tell anyone in fear she would find out, so it stands to reason you must have told someone else. Even if not the force."

Teresa was far from stupid, and she instantly knew what was happening. She knew that this was the main reason he was talking to her. She may be in danger, but he also suspected her.

There *was* one other person, though.

"Wait, you know Sally Noland?" she said.

"Should I?"

"She must've been with the force for thirty years. She's kind of a den mother to all the women at the precinct."

Frank shook his head, the name not ringing a bell.

"She wears a leg brace," Teresa added. "Always got a cane and—"

"Oh wait, gray-haired, heavy set?"

"Heavy set?" Teresa repeated, deadpanning. "Really?"

"What? She *is*, right? What about her?"

"Her father was a cop. All her brothers were cops. She's a sergeant but not on the streets anymore. She's been in the records library since her accident a decade ago."

"You told her about it?" Frank asked.

"Not really. She saw Jack grab my ass when he thought no one else was around. Came up to me later, chewed me out for sleeping with such a sleazeball. Begged me to break it off as he wasn't good enough for me. But I, of course, denied it. Carried on as usual. I never told her anything, though. Didn't confirm or deny it. Just walked away. As I said I *only* ever told my sister."

. . .

Pulling up outside his apartment, Frank took a set of keys from his pocket and handed them over to Teresa, who was sitting in the passenger seat.

"Here's the key. Apartment 4E. Lock yourself in, okay?"

He continued as she took the keys. "I'll phone before I come back so you can be sure it's me. I'll ring twice and hang up, then ring again. Don't answer the phone for anyone else. Don't open the door. Don't even look out of the window. Go in. Shut the curtains. I'll go to the station and pick up your bag from your locker. I'm guessing you got a change of clothes in there?"

"Yeah. It's locker 435," she replied in a bit in a daze after what happened. "Are you going to see if Sally is on?"

"Don't worry about that now. Just go in, get a shower. There's a clean dressing gown on the back of the bathroom door. You can wear that till I get back with your clothes. And there's food in the fridge. Help yourself."

After saying goodbye, Teresa stood in the vestibule leading to Frank's apartment. As soon as she stepped inside and was safely in the building, Frank pulled away in his car.

Chapter 6

The police precinct was quiet as Frank walked through the foyer, past the front desk, and down the corridor leading to the locker rooms.

On the way, he stopped at a soda machine, threw in two dollars, and waited for his chosen can to drop. He was fully aware of how much alcohol he had drunk, coupled with how little he had eaten. His breath must have reeked of whiskey.

The can opened with an effervescent fizz, and he started to drink it. Swooshing the cherry flavor around his mouth. On the third gulp, he gargled before swallowing, then dropped the half full can in the nearby trash.

He remembered what his ex-wife once called him, and it was the reason for their breakup. She called him a "robotic alcoholic." No feelings and fueled by booze.

He could not really argue that or blame her for leaving him.

Pushing open the locker room door, Frank crossed through the male area, where some cops were off duty, swapping their uniforms for their civilian clothing. He paid them no mind as he walked through and up to the door that had a big sign plastered on it that read *NO ADMITTANCE.*

Ignoring it, he walked through to the cleaner's corridor and across to another door leading to the female locker rooms.

"What the hell ya doin' in here, McCrae?" the deputy chief, halfway through undressing, shouted as she noticed him walking in.

"Passing through, ma'am," he replied, averting his eyes.

"You a peeping tom or something?" another woman asked.

"Sorry, got an emergency," he said, making a beeline for the end of the room, where number 435 sat. Opening the locker with haste, Frank reached in and grabbed Teresa's rucksack.

Turning back, he paused as he approached the deputy chief. "Ma'am," he said, his gaze intently locked to the floor. "Would you know if Seargent Sally Noland's on duty in records?"

"How the hell would I know? Get out of here!"

. . .

With Teresa's rucksack over one shoulder, Frank got out of the elevator on the second floor. He walked through the glass double doors and into the main record library offices. It was a large room lined with shelves of archive folders and banks of microfiche stations along one side and a long run of glass walled offices on the other. It was a place that smelled of old paper. A smell Frank didn't like.

Any other officer would have waited to come here till morning, but if there was even a slim chance that one of his questions could be answered, Frank had to at least try. Not like he needed sleep at the moment. He was beyond tired and fully into his tenth wind of the day.

As the strip lights buzzed softly above his head, he could hear a *tap, tap, tap* coming from an area beyond the bookshelves.

It was Sally Noland.

He may not have known her name before tonight, but he knew that sound. Whenever he had to come down here, he would hear it. The *tap, tap, tap* of her cane as she hobbled around, filing reports among the archive shelves.

Peering into the main room, Frank saw her. Dressed in a police uniform, with one leg set in a permanent brace, she walked with a cane. One that *tap, tap, tapped* on the floor tiles. In her fifties, with gray close-cropped hair and a stocky physique, she looked like a sad person.

Catching his gaze, she nodded politely as she walked across to the other side of the room, to where the reception desk sat.

"Can I help you?" she asked as she turned and perched on the desk's stool.

Her demeanor was dour and tired.

"You're here late," Frank said with a friendly smile as he walked over.

"Yeah, well, when you guys stop needing old case files urgently, then maybe I can stop having to do shifts to keep this room open twenty-four seven," she retorted, unamused. "Now, what can I help you with? You're homicide, right? McCrae?"

"Yeah, I think we have a mutual friend."

"Doubt that."

"I guess we should really know each other better," Frank's charm hit into overdrive with his whiskey blood pumping, his smile kind and friendly. A far cry from the gruff, sober, unapproachable exterior he would normally have in the day time. "We've probably passed each other in the halls for years. Guess we were both too busy to say hello?"

"Hello," she replied, her expression not shifting. "You said we had a friend in common? Who?"

Frank smiled, knowing that his friendly approach was not going to work here. Sally was obviously made of much stronger stuff.

"Officer Mallory?" he replied, keenly observing any reaction she may have.

But he got one that he did not expect. A smile. In his mind, she could very well be in league with the killer and was expecting a twitch or a look of shock or anything that said *Oh, shit*, but that is not what he saw.

"Oh, Teresa." She grinned. "Yeah, she's a fine girl. How is she? Haven't seen her in a while."

As Frank spoke, his words were carefully chosen but came out as conversational and off-the-cuff. "She's okay—now anyway. She had a close call tonight. Too close."

"Oh no!" Sally said, surprised. "What happened?"

"She was working undercover, looking into the Ellen Forrest murder," he lied. "Ran into a real sonofabitch. Her backup was also taken out. It was a mess."

"Ellen Forrest?" Sally said, looking genuinely worried. "But Teresa's okay, though, right?"

"Resting at the hospital, couple of broken bones," Frank lied again. "Ward C, if you wanna visit in the next couple of days."

"Thank the lord!" she said, glancing upward for a moment. "She's a lovely girl."

"We'll it's nice to have met you. We should all grab a beer sometime."

"That would be lovely," she replied.

Through Frank's friendly smile, he had sized this officer up. His instinct told him that she knew something. That she was lying. About something. That she was the one thread that was loose. *Wasn't she?* He had no idea how, but his gut was screaming at him that something about her was very off.

"We'll, I'll leave you to it," he said, with a knock of his hand on the desk. "Just thought I'd say hi."

As he left the precinct, he made his way to the parking lot, then sat in his car, waiting.

If his gut was right, Sally would leave work soon, despite her shift not ending till morning. She would want to go and tell this psycho where Teresa was. She would not risk calling him from the station. That would be a rookie move. No, his money was that she would leave and tell that maniac in person. And if she was not in cahoots with him and had just prank called Ellen Forrest out of some misguided way to help Teresa get her man, then she would probably still leave her shift early, terrified of being found out, and go straight to the hospital to confess to Teresa her part in all this.

And there she was. Sally Noland. Hobbling on her cane across the parking lot, she looked worried as she got into her car, not without difficulty due to her brace and quickly drove away.

Sally's car sped out of the 14th Street Midtown South precinct and, after hitting the Henry Hudson Parkway, drove south, past a multitude of piers along the

Hudson River shoreline, where large container ships worked all night to load and unload their goods.

But not all piers were awake with stevedores toiling around the clock. Pier 14, once part of what was a bustling maritime economy, had fallen into disuse. It stood as a derelict reminder of what once was. A few years earlier, this pier had been used as a place to stage avant-garde art shows, where bohemian crowds would venture under cover of night and stage impromptu exhibitions and events. But even those times had gone. The pier stood as a graffitied, decrepit eyesore on the water's edge.

As Sally's car pulled up to the gates of the pier, she hobbled out of her car, unlocked it, and drove through. Frank knew this only meant one thing, that his gut was right. Sally Noland was involved in all of this. She was going to see the maniac.

Through the darkness, Frank had trailed her with his headlights switched off, holding back a few hundred yards on the street. But he could tell from the way she was driving, she was not used to this kind of activity. She did not take her time to appear under the radar. She had bolted along the parkway twenty miles over the speed limit, not a way to stay unnoticed. She had been lucky a patrol car hadn't spotted and pulled her over.

And the fact she did not close or lock the gate to Pier 14 behind her? A telltale sign of panic—and one Frank McCrae was damn glad of. He was too old to be scaling fences at the docks in the middle of the night. No, now he could just park his car along the verge of the parkway and venture in by foot.

As he walked through the entrance to the pier, Frank hugged the darkness as he snapped his gun from his holster. He had lost sight of Sally after she drove through the gate so crept through as quietly and alert as possible.

Ahead, silhouetted in the murky darkness, were the gigantic skeletal remains of the warehouse. Once home to cargo from many a great ship, it now lay in decay.

Outside the warehouse, he soon noticed Sally's car parked up with the driver's side door still wide open. She obviously could not wait to get in there.

High above, the storm clouds were still as pendulous as they had been all week, but the threat of the rain was greater. The clouds let out a foreboding rumble as if they were getting angry at the city below, ready to unleash fury upon it.

The air remained humid and sticky as a noise from inside the large rotten warehouse caught Frank's ear. Heavy limped footsteps, hitting wood in a hurry. Sally.

Through the broken slats of the warehouse's roof, the moonlight that managed to break through the threatening storm clouds, flitted down into this immense and hollow space, giving it an ethereal silver hue.

Stepping through a splintered hole in the wall,

Frank could smell not just the rot but the animal waste that lay around. Scanning the floorboards, he could see an abundance of rat droppings. So many that he knew this building had to be infested and from the smell. It was a current plague, not historical.

Careful to not make a sound and not tread in the rancid feculence, Frank could feel the thousands of red rat eyes that, no doubt, stared at him from the shadows. He could deal with spiders. He could deal with snakes. But rats? Rats were creatures that gave him the creeps. Disease on tiny legs. Given a choice, he would have left as soon as he saw the droppings, but what he was doing was greater than his own discomfort.

Dipping behind a huge empty, damp wooden crate, Frank peered out into the main expanse of the warehouse. The whole building was covered with large white signs. Upon them, bold, red letters spelled *DANGER*. These were on wooden ladders. Walls. Platforms. Everywhere . . . . Even on the floors, where the wooden boards had crumbled away, exposing the river below, icy cold and black as the night itself. From the sheer number of warning signs on display, it seemed nowhere in this building was safe. And having followed Sarah Noland, the signs seemed to be screaming their warnings directly at him. Telling him of the danger he was walking into, not about the rotten wood they had been attached to.

As he tried his best to silence every creak that sounded from under his feet, Frank soon heard a muffled talking coming from up ahead. Beyond a large tower of crates, he could only just hear the voice but could tell it was Sally Noland's.

"I told you to do this *one* thing for me, to take her and not hurt her," she said in hushed tones as if aware she was being watched. "We could have ended it tonight. Hidden her away and waited for them to blame that other cop. But she got away."

Frank then spotted Sally through a narrow gap between two piles of crates.

She continued. "You know I love you. I will *always* love you. But it's all going too far. You just wanted the mayor and commissioner, right? You wanted your revenge on them but then you . . . You hurt all those other people. And I'm trying to fix it. I'm *trying* to help you. That's what the plan was from after the first one. I found that cop to take the fall. Someone they could believe had done it. But you kept on. You kept killing . . . . I'm not even sure the plan will work anymore. I'm not sure it would ever have worked. But now she's in a hospital probably telling everyone who you are."

Frank kept his breathing as shallow as possible as he peered between the crates, trying to see who Sally was talking to, but all he could see was a shoulder. A very large shoulder in a police uniform.

It's him.

He moved in closer, trying to see as much as he could.

Sally reached out and grabbed this figure's gloved

hand. Then, as she held it tenderly, she slowly removed the glove.

Frank nearly gasped loudly, giving away his position as he saw the figure's large, horribly scarred hand. Lined with dry gouges through its flesh, long thick twine had been crudely dug through the hand, seemingly stitching it together like a human patchwork doll.

Lifting the monstrously butchered hand to her lips, Sally gently kissed it.

"I know you have such anger in you," she said quietly as if it were pillow talk between them. "But I thought it would be the dealers and the junkies and the human filth that you'd be cleaning the city of, like before. Wiping the dirt from our streets. But . . . you took those poor people." She kissed his hand again before continuing. "I wish I knew what you were thinking, Matty. I really do."

Finally, a name! Frank thought as he continued to eavesdrop.

"I said I'd stick by you, and I will. But please . . . Do me this one thing . . . No more innocents?" She stared up at the figure lovingly. "For me? I can't cover up anymore. I can't get blood on my hands again. I just can't."

Done wrong? Frank's mind reeled with possibilities. *So, could this be a cop who was thrown off the force and now he was getting revenge? But why was he listening to Sally? Why was he silent? What are those scars?*

As he thought about all of this, he stared at the sheer size of the man. Though he could only partially see him through the crates, Frank could tell that the man's shoulder was at least at his head height, and with Frank being six-foot-one, this put this cop at nearly seven-foot-tall, if not more.

Before Frank could hear anymore, a large, muck-covered rat scurried out from the crate in front of him, darting directly past his shoes, causing him to jerk his foot backward in fear. As he did, his sole scraped against the wet wooden floorboard, emitting a loud squeak.

"Who the hell's there?" Sally called out, alerted to his presence. "Answer me!"

Frank held as still as he could.

Without warning, a gunshot suddenly shattered the silence.

BAM!

The bullet whizzed past Frank, smashing into a pile of rotten timber nearby. His pulse raced, but he held firm. Controlling his breathing as best he could. The bullet missed him by only a few inches. He knew that the cop didn't fire the shot. He could see that man's hands through the crates. It was Sally.

Then two more shots were fired.

BAM! BAM!

Putting away her still smoking gun, Sally quickly grabbed a small flashlight from her handbag and pointed it into the darkened warehouse from where the squeak came from. The beam passed over the crates that shielded Frank's presence.

"Probably a rat," she then murmured, staring into the darkness.

Frank, having closed his eyes tightly, had braced himself for the possible bullet hit that never came. When he finally got the nerve to open his eyes again, he noticed that the large man was no longer standing in front of Sally.

"Matty?" Sally called out. "Don't leave me. Please!" She paused, becoming overcome with desperation, causing her words to tremble. "I need you . . . And *you need me*, Matty . . . Come back!"

But he had gone, and she was left in the dark, holding her flashlight in one hand and his white glove in the other.

Frank had to get out of there before she saw him. The last thing he wanted was for her to realize that she had been followed and that her role in this had been uncovered.

Quietly sneaking out of the warehouse, Frank hurriedly made his way past her car and out of the gate. The same way he had come in. With each breath, he prayed that she was walking slowly and he could get out, unseen.

Reaching his car, he allowed himself a moment to breathe as he grabbed the keys from his pocket and holstered his gun.

Behind him, a large hand reached and grabbed him by the shoulder.

Whirling in one quick movement, Frank expertly pulled out his gun from the holster and pointed it at the uniformed man.

"What w-were you doing in there?" the night watchmen said as he stared, terrified at Frank's gun.

Quickly realizing, Frank lowered his weapon and smiled apologetically at the watchman. "I'm a cop."

"Y-You shouldn't be in there," the watchman uttered nervously. "You can get yourself killed. It's dangerous. Place is falling apart."

"I needed to take a leak. What can I say?" Frank shrugged. "Sorry for the gun."

The watchman nodded, still shook. "Bit jumpy tonight, huh?"

Frank continued. "I saw the uniform . . . Not the best thing to see at the moment."

"Next time, piss somewhere else," the watchman said, walking away.

That night had been intense. In fact, the whole week had been the most stress Frank had felt on the job in decades. Getting in the car and putting the keys in the car's ignition, he didn't drive off just yet. Instead, he sat in darkness, intensely staring at the pier's gate.

He didn't have to wait long as Sally's headlights soon broke through the darkness and her car came tearing out the pier and turned down the parkway.

As that happened as if cutting through the tension,

the storm clouds at last relented as a sudden clap of thunder shattered the air with an immense boom. No longer a distant rumble, this was a city-shaking roar. And after teasing the city for far too long, the rain began to pour heavily. It came down in relentless torrents, hammering down ferociously.

Unlike most of the people of New York, Frank did not welcome the downpour. Rain was no ally to a cop. It washed away evidence, blurred timelines, and complicated cases. Rain was a persistent adversary, one he could do without. Especially with a case like this.

After a restless night spent on his couch, leaving his bed to Teresa, Frank was up and out early. He had made no mention to her of what he had seen, only advising her to stay at his place for rest. His focus was singular: to get back to the records library before Sally's night shift began.

Now, in the hushed stillness of the library, Frank fixed his gaze on the computer screen. His team had already compiled a list of officers and former officers fitting the Maniac Cop's description, narrowing it down to eleven suspects. Yet each had a solid alibi, and none bore the name Matt, Matthew or anything remotely similar.

It was sheer happenstance that Frank had no idea

what he was doing with searching the database and had submitted a search query so vague that it returned results he had not seen before. His search was for anyone named Matthew who was six foot ten or taller and nothing else.

The system had thrown up two results. One was a man who had been injured in an industrial accident, seventy years old and hooked up to constant life support, and the other . . . the other not only matched the basic search criteria, but this person was also a member of the NYPD.

MATTHEW CORDELL

Born: 7th August 1947
Occupation: NYPD Officer (18th Precinct)
Arrest Date: 1st August 1976
Agency: Internal Affairs Division, NYPD
Incarceration Date: 18th August 1976 (SSCF)
Incarceration Term: LWOP
Charges:
- Murder (2nd Degree) 5 counts
- Excessive Use of Force (Multiple Counts)
- Violation of Civil Rights (Title 18, U.S. Code, Section 242)
- Misuse of Authority (Abuse of Power)
- Tampering with Evidence
- Assault with Intent to Cause Serious Bodily Harm

- Unlawful Retaliation Against Fellow Officers (Obstruction of Justice)

But when Frank looked at the last line section of the report, his heart sank.

Deceased: 19th October 1976 (SSCF)
Cause of Death:
Primary
- Traumatic Brain Injury
- Haemorrhagic Shock
Contributing
- Multiple Penetrating Injuries
- Multiple Defensive Injuries

"Shame what happened to Matty," came the old voice from behind him. "He didn't deserve what happened."

Turning from the screen, Frank saw Officer Clancy, one of the other record officers. Even when Frank joined the force decades ago, Clancy worked down here, and he looked old even back then.

"Matty?" Frank asked.

"If you got time to read, I got a load of old press cuttings and reports about him you can look at?"

Frank turned to the screen, then back up to Clancy. "He's dead, right?"

Clancy nodded, forlorn. "Wanna see what we have on him?"

Frank should have said no. He could have dismissed this based on the evidence at hand, but something made him want to learn more. Besides, being declared dead meant little. Reports could be falsified. Logs amended. Just because a machine says you are buried underground doesn't mean you died. What if this Cordell faked his death and disappeared? And was getting revenge on those who put him away?

Clancy kept talking as he grabbed a ladder and climbed up to a high shelf of thick leather binders. "Matty was old-school. He believed in the old saying, 'Shoot first and ask questions later.' But he was a good guy. Was kind to me, gentle enough if you got to know him." He shrugged. "Just looked like a beast and acted like one if you were breaking the law."

Finding the relevant folder, he pulled it off the shelf, then took it to the table next to Frank.

"Before we got them all scanned for the microfiche, we had to cut out press clippings that were about the NYPD." Opening the book on the table, Clancy turned to Frank. "Here is what we have about Matty. I put them all in the one place after it started to become a regular occurrence. No one's looked at these since he died."

The open pages had three news articles glued onto them. "Mafia Chief Slain By NYPD Officer," "Supercop Raids Terrorist Facility . . . Kills Six," and "Officer Kills East Village Rapist."

As Frank looked at the headlines, the word "kill" stood out. Repeatedly.

"All those were Matty," Clancy said. "He was an idol to many on the force."

"Were you friends?"

Clancy smiled. "I don't think Matty had any friends. But he was nice to me. And I hate to admit it, but he used to like to come in here and look at these clippings, just like you're doing now. I think he liked being a celebrity. Liked being known. Probably liked being feared a bit, too. They only reported the ones he killed, though. Not the hundreds he arrested. More sensationalist like that." Clancy took a sharp intake of breath. "Such a shame."

Turning the page. There were more articles about Cordell. More about him stopping crime with a deadly force. Never talk of other cops being involved. Just him. Page after page of the same.

Then, on the last page, the headline was bigger. Bolder.

OFFICER INDICTED.

The subheading was just as striking.

DECORATED OFFICER CHARGED ON
MULTIPLE COUNTS.

"They sent him down for doing his job," Clancy

said. "It was wrong what they did. Putting him in Sing Sing with all the rapists and murderers that he put away. No wonder he didn't even make it a couple of months."

"The computer said he was also charged for violation of civil rights. Is that 'cause he killed a lot of them?"

Clancy almost shouted his reply. "They *murdered* him. Those bastards had it out for him and sent him down!"

Frank stared down at the article. "Did he have any kids? Widow? Or married to the job like me?"

Clancy sighed. "He had a girl. She was a cop, too. I think they were gonna marry if . . . if what happened never happened. But that's a sad story, too."

"Yeah?"

"Right after he was convicted, the poor girl took a jump out of a window, trying to kill herself. Terrible thing for a Catholic girl like her to do. Crippled herself."

"Let me guess, Sally Noland?"

"Yeah." Clancy nodded. "After her accident, she asked to be transferred to here. Guess it reminded her of him. She'll be in later today. Her shift starts at six, if you wanna ask her about it? She loves talking about Matty, even this long after."

Frank left the records library in a daze. Did Cordell fake his death? If so, how? Was it a cover up?

All evidence clearly pointed to the Maniac Cop being him, but was that even possible?

He remembered seeing the man's hands at the pier. The scarred, stitched hands. And also that fact that both he and Teresa shot him. Could he be—

No.

That was impossible.

He had to go home and speak to Teresa. She would be the only one who would believe this story. This insane story.

Chapter 7

Jack Forrest was back in the interrogation room, handcuffed to the table.

He had been held in a cell for days now, waiting for the police to come to their senses. To discover he was innocent of all he had been accused of.

He would probably have got very angry at being arrested if it were not for his guilt. With Ellen, he may have been innocent of physically murdering her, but he blamed himself for her death, nevertheless. If he hadn't had an affair, if he hadn't gone to that hotel, if he had just stayed home like she begged him, she would have lived. As it stood, he didn't hold the knife, but he was to blame.

When he tried to figure it out and who could be setting him up, his thoughts always came back to Ellen. To the crime scene photos that the investigators had shown him. Images he could never unsee. Sure, people have affairs all the time for many reasons—marriages break down—but those facts did nothing to lessen the emotional turmoil he was in. And knowing Ellen, if she was up in heaven, looking down, she would have been glad that he was going through this.

He waited in the interrogation room for Teresa. She had called last night to tell him that she was working with Frank McCrae, the man investigating his case, and they had made progress, and they needed to tell him in person what they found.

Teresa, she was the other half of Jack's pain. He could not help that he loved Ellen, just as much as he could not help that he loved Teresa, too. If he could change his heart, he would have.

Frank and Teresa, with their police badges clipped to the lapels of their civilian jackets, had managed to avoid being drenched by the storm that raged outside. Only a few stray drops of rain dotted their jackets as they descended the stairs to cell block and interrogation rooms.

Walking along the brightly lit corridor, they soon noticed the duty guard standing watch outside one of the dozen interrogations rooms, waiting for them.

"This Jack Forrest?" Frank asked the guard as he pointed to the room.

"How long d'you need, Detective?" the guard replied.

"An hour maybe."

"Okay,. Just buzz when you're done, and I'll let you out." The guard opened the door, letting them inside.

As the door was closed and the guard out of sight, Teresa had run around the table and hugged Jack, whose cuffed hands stopped him being able to return the gesture.

"It's so good to see you, babe," Jack said with an emotional smile, almost teary as he looked at her.

"We know who the killer is," she blurted, unable to contain her excitement.

"Sit," Frank said to her as he took one of the seats on the other side of the table.

"What do you mean?" Jack replied, staring at her, then to Frank, aghast. "Really?"

Frank nodded. "We think so."

"Did you tell the DA? The commissioner?"

Teresa, sitting down next to Frank, reached over and held Jack's cuffed hands. "They wouldn't believe us if we just went and told them, not yet. You won't either."

"What are you talking about?"

Frank cleared his throat and leaned forward, speaking in a measured tone. "Did you know an officer from a decade ago from the eighteenth called Matthew Cordell?"

"Met him? That was before my time," Jack replied.

"Heard of him, though. That's that trigger-happy guy, right? From the seventies? Killed all those crooks."

Frank nodded. "I never met him either. Knew there was a cop who was sent down. But I tend to not pay attention to anything out of my purview. But from what I've read, he shot a *lot* of bad guys when he was on the beat. Murderers, terrorists, pedophiles, gang bosses. You name it. He took em down. Arrested them if he couldn't get a kill shot. When that Eastwood movie *Dirty Harry* came out in '78, I read something earlier that insinuated that it was based on him."

"Well, what about him? Does he know anything?"

"Not quite," Teresa said. "Cordell went to jail . . . Sent to Sing Sing. He died in jail in '76."

"Uh . . . what?"

Jack had no idea where this was going.

"So, let's suppose he didn't die, okay?" Frank added.

"Okay?"

"Let's suppose he's back after all these years?" Frank continued. "Only this time . . . he's killing the innocent and not the guilty."

Jack thought for a second. None of this lined up for him.

"How does that make sense? Are you saying he's a zombie or something? Or he just didn't die and faked it? And why would he kill innocent people if he was all about killing the bad guys? And most of all—and this is the ten-thousand-dollar question—why me? I never met the guy. Sounds like bullshit."

"I saw whoever it was, Jack," Teresa said. "Frank and I both did."

"What?! How about you lead with that and not about a dead cop."

"He grabbed me," she said, her voice wavering. "I can still feel his hands on me. They were cold, clammy hands. I've had to touch a few dead people in my life. *That's* what he felt like. He didn't feel alive."

"We are *not* saying he's a zombie," Frank cut in sternly.

"Well, what *are* you saying?"

"We're saying that the killer is Matthew Cordell. How and why? We got no idea. I shot that bastard square in the chest multiple times—"

"And I shot him in the head," Teresa added. "Twice."

"Despite that, he kept on coming at us." Frank took a breath, not quite believing his own words. "Jack, we got no answers for you about this. We just know what we saw, what we did. I've got an appointment in the morning at Sing Sing with the Chief Medical Officer, Dr. Felix Gruber. He was around back in '76 and signed Cordell's death certificate. He may be able to shed light on all this insanity if he remembers any of it."

Jack nodded. Not knowing what to think.

"We'll sort it out," Frank added. "There has to be a rational explanation to everything."

"Thanks for believing me," Jack said. "And believing Teresa."

Frank nodded and then checked his watch. It was 6:34 p.m. "Officer Mallory?" he said as he stood from the table. "I'll be back in a bit. You continue questioning the suspect for a while, okay?" He gave her a knowing wink.

"Thank you," Teresa said, glad to finally have some time alone with Jack.

A minute later, Frank had left as the guard remained outside the door.

"Can I kiss you?" Teresa asked hesitantly.

"Why you even asking? Of course you can."

Uneasily she shifted in her chair. "Because of Ellen," she murmured. "I mean, it's understandable if it's too soon or—"

"Let's not kid ourselves. What I did was bad. The way I went behind her back . . . she deserved better than that. Better than *me*. I can admit that I was a coward. Ellen and I weren't in love anymore. Hadn't been for a long time. We stayed together because it was easy, because we didn't know how to leave. But being in here, I've had enough time to think about it all. And there's one thing I know for certain." He leaned forward across the table, his eyes locked on Teresa's. "I love you, and I mean that. Not just the words. I really do."

"I love you, too," she replied. "And I never got the chance to say how sorry I was. For everything. For my part in it all."

"Your part? You had nothing to do with what happened. It was between me and her."

Teresa leaned to meet Jack halfway over the table and gave him a tender kiss on the lips. "I guess if we catch this guy, it'll be better," she said. "We'll have done right by her."

"Do you *really* believe this Cordell stuff? I get you both saw the guy—"

"Every time he mentions Cordell, I doubt it as well. I get that sick feeling, like I'm a fool for believing it. But I can't ignore all the evidence or what I saw. No matter how it all sounds."

It was past the shift change in the records library. Clancy would have left, and Sally Noland should have taken over. Frank was not sure she would even turn up for her duty but needed to take that chance. He needed to speak to her again, knowing all he had discovered. She had to be confronted but on his terms, when she did not expect it.

From all he knew of her, she was emotionally attached to the killer, which meant she probably had no choice but to help him.

Walking out of the elevator that led to the library, Frank could hear the clacking of a keyboard coming from a computer terminal. Walking around to come up to the terminal from behind, Frank noticed that the place was deserted aside from Sally, who sat at a computer searching the police records.

"Hello," he said.

Sally jolted with surprise.

Before she could reply, Frank sat himself on a chair next to her and motioned to the computer. "When did you learn to work one of these?"

"Uh, they sent all records staff back to school to learn the programs a couple of years ago."

Frank smirked. "Well, they ought to send you back to the firing range."

"What are you talking about?"

"You missed me by a mile," Frank said. "Last night. On the pier."

Sally's face dropped.

Noticing what was on the screen, Frank may not know a thing about computers, but he could tell what she was looking at, the deployment names for the special task force that had been set up to capture the Maniac Cop. And his name was right at the top of the list. Task Force Investigator: Detective Lieutenant Frank McCrae.

"Still keeping him posted?" Frank asked, his smile not faltering, his demeanor creepily upbeat considering what he was saying.

Sally was shocked into silence. She stared at him like a deer in headlights.

Looking down, Frank noticed her handbag. Without asking, he grabbed it and peered inside. As the leather opened up, sitting on top of her purse was a shock of white fabric. A white ceremonial police glove. The one he saw Sally take last night.

Her breathing stilted as she let out a tiny whimper, watching Frank take the glove and try it on. Like a child putting on an adult coat, it was far too big. Frank could fit in two of his fingers into each one of the glove's.

"A little on the large side for you, wouldn't you say, Sally?" he said as he then took the glove off and handed it back to her.

On the verge of tears, she snatched it back and grasped it tightly to her chest.

"He'll think I let him down," she said, her voice cracking as her distress began to grow. Her hands trembled as she held the glove, her gaze fixed upon it as if it were the love of her life. "He'll think I snitched on him."

"Sally, listen to me." Frank's words were calm but his smile had gone. His expression was deadly serious as he spoke. He knew that confronting a woman in love would do nothing. He had to try a different approach. He had to reassure her. "You were the loyal one, Sally," he said, intentionally reusing her name and complimenting her intent, all to establish a connection between them. To show her he was not a bad man here and that he was on her level. "You stood by him no matter what he did. Who he killed. I heard you last night. You didn't want that, right? You want him to stop. You're a good person."

Sally weakly shook her head. "No, I'm not."

"Sally, you know he's crazy, don't you?"

She did not answer, just looked lost as she gripped his glove tighter.

"If it's Matt Cordell you loved all those years ago," Frank continued, "what he is now . . . there's nothing left of Cordell, is there?"

"He just wants to kill. He's so angry," she said, maudlin. "I helped him. But I didn't want people to die. I tried to stop it. To get him to cover his tracks. And at first, he did . . . Then he just kept on and on. The anger . . . He . . ." Sally looked at Frank as a tear fell down her cheek. "He'll kill me, you know? For talking. But I don't know what to do. It's getting worse." She stared at her hands, feeling ashamed of all she had done. "You were there last night—you saw him? Why didn't you make a move?"

"One old cop with one old gun against a woman in love and a man who . . . a man like him. I wouldn't have stood a chance, not then. But next time. *Next* time, I will."

Sally fell silent again.

"Why does he listen to you?" Frank asked. "You

say you tried to help him cover his tracks, and he listened. How?"

Sally shook her head. "I've got no idea. I don't know why. Maybe he wants to do the right thing? But his anger won't let him. Since Sing Sing, he hasn't spoken. He hasn't been Matty."

"Can I ask, did you put Ellen Forrest's body in that motel? That didn't seem like a thing he'd do, judging by how he left his other victims."

Sally looked guiltily at him. Despite her not confirming it, Frank knew that she had helped Cordell more than she let on. It was then he realized that it was Sally who knocked out Officer Malone as he waited in the sedan, not the Maniac Cop. Maybe he didn't intend to let Teresa live after all? Maybe he wasn't trying to take her? Maybe she just got lucky. Before he could ask more questions, Sally broke down.

"I can't help you. I can't. *I can't,*" she blubbed.

"You're the *only* one who can, Sally." Frank reached his hand forward and placed it on her shoulder comfortingly. "You can help me stop him from hurting more innocent people. We can make sure he's taken into custody without another person dying. Isn't that what you want? For him to be safe? For this to stop?"

"No, no," she whimpered. "I just want my Matty back."

"I heard you say that he wanted revenge—but at what cost? Is his anger worth killing people who had no part in it? He killed a woman walking home from work.

A young guy on his way home with his girlfriend. A musician—"

"Stop, Stop! I can't hear it anymore!"

Up in the interrogation room, Teresa and Jack were deep in conversation as she still held his cuffed hands over the table.

"You know what?" she said with a hopeful smile. "Despite all this. There's gotta be some way of—"

A muffled yelp sounded from the corridor outside.

"What the hell was that?" Jack murmured.

"Was that someone screaming?" she added as she let go of his hands and stood. Stepping toward the door, she peered through its small viewing window. Looking in all the directions, she could not see much with its restricted view.

"I can't see the guard," she said. "Guess he went on a break?"

Quickly her finger found the red call button on the wall.

"I'm sure it's okay," Jack proffered, but Teresa pressed the button anyway, sensing something off out there.

That buzzer should have called the guard to open the door within seconds, but no one came.

She buzzed it again. For longer this time.

"Why doesn't anybody answer?" she muttered.

Then the door *clicked* as the lock was released. The sound echoing in the silence.

She turned to Jack with an apprehensive expression.

Still, no guard appeared.

Her hand gripped the door handle and slowly pushed down. It opened with ease as she pulled it toward her.

Quickly having a second thought, she turned and walked back over to Jack, rummaging in her pocket.

"Something's not right," she said. "We gotta move." She then produced her keys from her pocket. Among them was a small silver key. She reached over and unlocked the cuffs.

Jack looked worried.

"What are you doing?" he whispered. "That'll just get me in more shit."

She freed his wrist and looked him dead in the eye. "You stay here, but I'm not leaving you cuffed. The guard's gone. We both heard a scream. I think this can be chalked up to extenuating circumstances."

He looked at her, unsure.

"And if it's all good, I'll come back and lock you right back in?"

She had fully taken charge and Jack, though, normally, the person leading found it inappropriately a turn on.

. . .

Opening the interrogation room door, Teresa peered out into the corridor before slowly and silently stepping out into the corridor.

At the end, toward the main holding cells of the precinct, was a guard's post. And there, sitting in a swivel chair, facing away from her, she could see the guard still on duty.

Breathing a sigh of relief, Teresa smiled as she shook her head. "Lazy bastard," she mumbled. "Hey," she called out, walking toward the guard's post. "What was that noise? We heard it from inside the room."

The guard didn't reply. He did not even turn around.

As she stepped closer, she noticed he did not move at all.

She reached out and grabbed the side of the chair. "Hey, I'm talking to you." As she turned the chair, the guard's body slumped forward, and his head, which had been balanced on his neck, tumbled off and landed to the tiles in front of her. The open neck wound pulsed out blood as if the head had kept the flow at bay.

Stifling a scream, Teresa held her mouth and backed away. She then saw the huge wet spatter of blood up the wall to the side of the desk. This had just happened.

The guard had not only been decapitated but the front of his chest had been butchered. Through the blood and viscera, she could clearly see the many,

many stab wounds. The barrage of this attack had been so great that the guard's smashed rib cage was visible through his horrifically slashed skin.

Teresa's brain spun with how this was possible. From the moment they heard the scream to coming out here was only a couple of minutes at most. How was such a brutal attack possible in such a short time?

Unable to contain his curiosity, Jack peered out from the interrogation room. As his eyes caught sight of Teresa, he then saw the guard's headless body.

Within moments, his flight mode kicked in.

"Teresa," he called out as he bolted from the room and down the corridor toward her. "We gotta go now!" He turned and looked to the holding cells beyond the locked, barred gate that stood in front of them. "Quickest way out is through there, and the gate's locked, so he must have gone the other way, right?"

The "he" Jack spoke of, they both understood, was Matt Cordell. The Maniac Cop. He was obviously here and after them.

Jack turned to the guard, to the large set of keys that hung from his belt. These, like the rest of this butchered man, had been covered in thick blood that still pumped rhythmically from his gaping throat tract.

Grabbing the keys from the guard's belt, Jack looked over the rest of the body. This guard had no holster, no cuffs, just the keys.

"Dammit," he said. "No gun."

"If anybody sees you running around with a gun,

you'll be shot," Teresa said as she took the keys from him and rushed over to the gate. "We just gotta go through, up the stairs, then we gotta go out through the offices." The key she tried didn't work, so she tried another. Then another.

"They're not gonna just let me out," Jack said, shocked as to what was happening.

"No," Teresa shook her head. "It's better to be surrounded by armed cops than down here alone."

The next key she tried worked. The barred gate clanked as its lock opened.

"Come on!" she said.

She didn't have to urge him. Jack was already beside her, pulling her through the gate by her arm.

Racing past the lines of dark, empty holding cells, they soon rounded a corner into the corridor that led to the staircase. Jack's breath came in a short, sharp gasp as his foot slipped on something slick, sending him crashing to the floor. Still holding his hand, Teresa tumbled, pulled down, and landed in a heap beside him.

They froze in shock at the sight before them.

A pair of legs blocked their path.

They dangled lifelessly from the ceiling.

Above them, the mutilated body of a policeman hung grotesquely. His abdomen had been torn open and his intestines pulled out and used to string him up to the light fixture. His body swayed on what was a grisly tether, blood and gore dripping steadily to the floor below. Spreading outward, staining Jack's shoes and splattering his trousers.

Frantically, they scrambled to their feet.

Jack stared at the horrific scene, his voice barely above a whisper. "What the fuck . . ." was all he could manage, his words hanging in the air like the very lifeless body before them. His eyes then traveled upward, catching on something strapped to the guard's belt. A holstered gun.

Gritting his teeth, he steeled himself, fighting back the revulsion rising in his gut. With an unsteady hand, he unclipped the holster, and he took the gun. Right then, a sickening squelch sounded. The body, with its intestine weakened by the strain, tore in half and gave way, plummeting to the floor. Jack narrowly had time to react as the corpse nearly fell on him, its dead weight hitting the ground with a moist squelch.

In the record library, Frank was still talking to Sally. She was just as upset, but the crying had stopped. She just stared at the glove in her hands with a sad look on her tear-stained face.

"Tell me how you contact him," he asked softly. "Is there a phone number? Or does he call you? Do you meet at a certain time each day? Does he stay at yours?"

This question made Sally laugh, a sad laugh, as she

took in short deep breaths to stop herself from crying again.

Slowly, she stood from the computer, grabbed her cane from resting on the edge of the table, then turned to walk away. "You really don't know anything, do you?"

"What do you mean?"

"You can't stop him," she said as she hobbled. "You don't find him. He just knows. He just knows where you are. I don't have to find him or tell him a thing. He just knows." She paused for a second as the tears came again. "He knows I'm no good to him anymore."

"Sally, come on," Frank pleaded as he stood to walk after her.

Before he could take another step, her tears turned to a desperate anger as she let out a shriek and whirled around, brandishing her cane up high.

Her cane then came down and smashed into the side of Frank's head, sending him crumpling to the floor.

As he fell heavily between two desks, Sally, once again, raised the cane above her head. Again and again, she brought her makeshift weapon down, smacking into his body. All he could do was shield his face from the blows by holding up his arm across it. He yelped in pain as the cane hit onto his arm and hip repeatedly.

After a dozen hits, Sally turned, then rushed away as fast as her leg brace and cane would allow her.

. . .

Up the murky stairwell from the holding cells, Jack gripped the gun, holding it up defensively as they walked. The thin, sporadic strip lights overhead flickered weakly as outside, the rain raged on, hammering against the small, barred windows in the stairwell, letting in only the darkness of the night.

Their movements were cautious, their footsteps slow and deliberate as they crept closer to ground level. Every creak and crack of the building made them freeze in place as they held their breaths. Every sound around them seemed amplified, the distant rumble of thunder, a groan of brickwork, and the relentless hammering of the rain on the glass.

They exchanged wary glances as they started up the last flight, and there, sprawled over the steps, was another body.

A policewoman heaped halfway down her head twisted back as she faced Jack and Teresa, with her body facing the other way. Her expression was stuck in a silent scream. As well as her neck, her arms and legs were also broken and jutted off in opposite angles.

"Just keep looking up," Jack whispered as he and Teresa slowly stepped around this body, trying to not focus on the full extent of the horror.

Only six more steps.

They were nearly to the top of the staircase.

Managing to avoid the mangled corpse that lay in their way, Jack and Teresa cautiously made their way to the double doors at the top of the flight.

. . .

Cautiously opening the doors, they walked through.

The brightly lit admin offices were empty.

The whole place was eerily silent. Though it was late, this building should always have some people working late at their desks.

Teresa glanced around, concerned.

"Where is everyone?" Jack asked.

Teresa silently motioned to the other side of the room, where the main entrance hall to the precinct was, separated by a glass partition wall.

Staring through this glass, they both gasped in shock.

In the entrance foyer, once a brilliant white glass-lined room, was a blood-soaked horror to behold.

Half a dozen officers, stabbed, bludgeoned, and torn into pieces. Their massacred remains lay in expanding pools of their own still-warm blood.

"How can one guy do this?" Teresa said, turning to Jack, unable to mask her nerves.

Jack could not answer. He just stared at the bloody mess beyond the glass.

Teresa's gaze moved beyond this scene and out to the front of the building, where she could just see Frank's car still parked up outside. "Hey, that's McCrae's car. He's gotta still be up in records. Let's go find him."

"No," Jack replied firmly. "You've been in danger

enough. Can't risk both of our lives. So, go to his car. If we're not out in five minutes, haul ass. You got me? You run and don't stop. I'll find him."

"What if Cordell found him first?"

"Either way. Five minutes."

Sally Noland rushed down the dark corridor toward the elevator, panicked and crying, as she hobbled as fast as she could. She quickly jammed the call button with her thumb.

"Please, please, please," she sobbed, willing the elevator to open. "Ple—"

She screamed as she was suddenly yanked backward. Two arms wrapped around her as she was dragged off her feet. Her cane pulled from her grasp.

She screamed as she saw him, Frank McCrae, with a bleeding gash on his head, gripping her tightly.

"Get off me," she yelled, unable to get a footing, as Frank dragged her back down the corridor.

A *ding* from the elevator suddenly caught both of their attention as its door slowly slid open.

Frank's eyes widened.

"No!" Sally screamed.

Inside the elevator, slumped in a bloody pile, was a policeman. A mass of torn flesh, broken bone, and contorted limbs. It was impossible to see which way the body was as it was all twisted into a surreal mess.

"He's here," Sally cried, more in fear than relief. "He's here for me!"

Her weight slumped into Frank's grip as she gave up the fight, resigned that her escape was thwarted.

Frank strained with all his might as he pulled her farther down the corridor, away from the elevator, away from the dead body. She offered no assistance or resistance, and he had to half drag, half carry her.

All she could do was cry uncontrollably. "I love you, Matty," she sobbed to no one. "I'm sorry I betrayed you."

Frank quickly glanced back to the elevator. To the dead body crumpled inside it. How could he beat someone who did that? Someone who did not react to bullets. He had only one choice. He had to hide somewhere safe until he could confront the man with an army of cops.

Reaching a clouded glass door to one of the side offices, Frank quickly reached out for the handle. Just as his finger touched the metal, the clouded panel around it shattered outward in a barrage of splintering glass as a huge, horrendously scarred hand burst through from inside.

In a second, this powerful hand pulled Sally out of Frank's grip right through the broken glass panel, lifting her into the air. Dragging her into the darkness of the office.

She screamed and gasped as she was pulled into the shadows.

Grabbing the gun from his holster, Frank kicked open the remains of the door and rushed after them.

"Freeze!" Frank shouted as he leveled his gun to the far end of the room. He could see the dark shadow of the Maniac Cop, which was terrifyingly illuminated from the light seeping in from the corridor.

Frank could not fully register what was happening.

Cordell had Sally by the throat, hoisting her into the air with one hand. Her feet dangled helplessly below, suspended nearly two feet from the floor. He held her as though she weighed nothing. She could only flail as she struggled to scream.

In his other hand, Cordell gripped his stiletto knife as he started to thrust it repeatedly into her chest. Over and over with an immense speed, his arm pounded the blade into her with such force that Frank could see the tip break out her back with each attack.

BANG!

Frank fired his gun, and the bullet slammed into Cordell's side.

The bullet did nothing. Cordell just continued to stab a few final times.

When this maniac cop was done, and with a singular ease, he flung the corpse of Sally across the room like a rag doll. It tumbled across the desks and slammed into the adjacent wall with a sickening thud.

Then he turned to Frank.

Bang! Bang! Two shots into Cordell's chest. Straight through the heart.

Bang! One to his shoulder.

Bang! Bang! Two to his head.

They hit.

They *all* hit.

But this maniac cop kept standing.

Turning sharply, Frank quickly bolted in the opposite direction, his heart pounding as his fear ballooned. Ahead, a row of glass office cubicles stretched out, their sleek partitions obstructing the most direct route to get to the staircase. These cubicles dominated the width of the room, forcing him to navigate a narrow, twisting path that wound around each one. He raced through them as quickly as he could.

But the Maniac Cop had no intention of diverting his course. He charged on after Frank, straight through the cubicles, smashing the glass panels with a brutal force, one after another. Hurling desks aside with a terrifying ease. The shattering and crashing sounds echoed like warfare, and the broken shards shot out in each direction, leaving a trail of destruction in Cordell's wake.

Frank, out of bullets, became overtaken by a sheer panic. His ragged breaths came in gasps as Cordell quickly closed the gap between them. Desperation then overtook him as he turned and hurled his empty pistol with all his might at the oncoming force. The weapon did nothing as it bounced harmlessly off Cordell's chest.

Next, Frank grabbed anything within his reach, a

chair, a typewriter, a desk lamp. Frank threw each of them wildly at Cordell, but each barely slowed the juggernaut. The chair splintered while the typewriter's reels snapped off, and the lamp bent as Cordell just continued toward him.

Rushing up the staircase, Jack heard the sudden screams and crashes coming from the offices above. Gun in hand, he rushed faster up the steps to the second-floor vestibule.

"McCrae," he shouted as he flung open the door to the record's library.

There was nowhere left to run.

Frank's escape had been cut short.

Where he had expected salvation, a door leading to the staircase, there was only a plain solid wall. The truth struck him like a sledgehammer: he had gotten turned around in the chaos. The exit wasn't here. It was in the next office down.

For a moment, the world seemed to hold its breath.

Then came the sound . . . heavy, deliberate footfalls echoing closer at speed.

The Maniac Cop was on him.

Frank turned with a look of desperation, but there was no escape, no second chances. Cordell towered over him, the long, bloodied blade in his hand.

It happened too fast for Frank to comprehend. The stiletto knife plunged into his chest like a shot, its tip slicing through his heart.

Frank McCrae, who had given everything to this job, fell down in this unremarkable, destroyed office. His knees buckled as the blade withdrew from his chest, slick and glistening. He fell back against the wall, leaving a streak of red where the blade had burst through his back.

Crouching, Cordell then thrust the blade at him again. Another colossal stab, this time into his neck.

Then another through Frank's cheek. With this stab, the blade crunched through his teeth and split his gums, slicing into his throat and out through the back of his head. The point collided with the wall behind with a *thunk* and stuck into the plaster. Blood erupted from out of his throat as Cordell yanked his blade back out.

As the Maniac Cop stood and backed away, Frank's hand trembled as it reached for something, *anything*, to help, but he found nothing.

This wasn't how it was supposed to end, he thought. He was the hero. *Aren't I?* He had fought too hard, survived too much to die in this way, in this place, at the hands of this monster. Yet here he was, fading into the darkness.

By the time Cordell reached out and picked up his body, Frank McCrae was gone.

. . .

Teresa felt lucky as she got out to Frank McCrae's car. He had left the driver's side door unlocked. Sitting inside, out of the rain that pelted down outside, her fingers tapped nervously on the wheel. She looked out at the precinct building, waiting for Jack and Frank to come scurrying out, hoping they would appear at any moment.

The street around her was empty. Aside from the rain, the whole place felt abandoned, like some kind of apocalypse had happened, and she was here stuck waiting in the car for people who may never come.

As she glanced at the dashboard clock, the seconds seemed to drag like hours. Something felt wrong, even with the bodies she had seen, knowing Cordell was in there, seemingly butchering everyone, the air felt even more oppressive as she waited.

Then a crash shattered high above, cutting through the sound of the surrounding storm.

Her heart leaped into her throat as her glance shot upward. From the second floor, she saw the window shatter outward, like jagged stars in the night, glittering as they rained down to the street level. A dark shadow followed them, tumbling toward her. It took a moment for her to process the horrifying truth of what it was.

Teresa's body moved before her mind caught up. She threw the door open and dove out onto the wet street, landing hard on her hands and knees.

Behind her, the car's roof crunched in with an

almighty smash of twisting metal and glass as the dark shadow collided heavily with it.

She turned, and with a look of terror on her face, she saw Frank McCrae's corpse slam through the crumpled roof and into the twisted wreckage.

Just as sudden as the crashing sound came, it then stopped. Leaving only the sound of rain.

She stared, horrified. If she had stayed in the car even a second longer, she would have been crushed beneath the weight.

"Oh my god . . ."

Her voice cracked as she crawled to her feet, her gaze locked on the scene in front of her. The car was beyond repair, and Frank's body was broken into the very metal it had collided with. Blood seeped into the creases of the vehicle, staining the remnants of the car seat fabric, then pooling on the pavement beneath it. Teresa couldn't tear her eyes away, as this was a man she trusted, a man who had saved her life from the Maniac Cop before and a man who promised to save both her and Jack. And he was here. Dead. Gone.

A cold dread then crept over her.

She could feel a stare at the back of her head.

Something there.

Something watching.

As she slowly turned around, she knew what she would see. There, at the window on the second floor, through the shattered glass, a figure looked back down at her. Matt Cordell. The Maniac Cop.

. . .

Minutes later, Jack moved cautiously through the wreckage of the records library offices. The space was a graveyard of shattered desks and overturned chairs. With his gun leading his way, his every sense was on high alert. Each footstep crunched against broken glass that littered the floor, creating an unnervingly loud sound in the silence.

"McCrae?" he whispered, taking a few steps farther. "Frank? You there?"

As he stepped through the jagged remnants of a glass partition, a sudden gust of wind brushed against his skin. Pulling his attention, he followed it to the source: a broken window at the other side of the room. Climbing over a splintered desk, he soon reached the jagged frame and peered out cautiously.

Jack's gaze dropped, drawn by the horrifying sight below. The crumpled car, its roof caved in. Blood pooling around a body that was slumped grotesquely within its wreckage. He then saw Teresa sobbing as she knelt on the street, staring at the wreckage.

"No," Jack whispered, his voice cracking as he realized who the body was.

It hit him like a physical blow, forcing him to recoil from the window as bile rose in his throat.

But Jack had no time to feel sick. Teresa was alone down there, vulnerable, and he *had* to get to her. He turned and sprinted back through the chaos of the office. Just as he was about to cross the threshold into the main corridor, a figure quickly emerged from the shadows.

Jack skidded to a halt, his gun instinctively snapping up. Breathless and caught off guard, he came face-to-face with Detective Lovejoy, who also had a gun and pointed it back toward Jack.

But unlike Jack, Lovejoy was shaking like a leaf. He had seen the devastation, seen the bodies and seen the gore. And he was face-to-face with Jack Forrest, a man, who, as far as he knew, was the maniac. A man who also brutally killed his own wife.

"All right, d-drop it," Lovejoy stuttered nervously. "P-Put your hands where I can see them. Back up against that wall."

"Whoa, whoa, hold on," Jack replied as he quickly moved his aim away from the detective. "I didn't do any of this. This wasn't me."

But Lovejoy kept his aim squared and stepped forward. "You b-broke out of your cell . . . you killed them all!"

"No, I *didn't* do this," Jack pled, stepping forward. "It wasn't me, it—"

"Stay where you are," Lovejoy shouted. "Don't move!"

Jack halted in his tracks and raised his hand. "Please, he's still here. You're letting him get away. We need to get—"

"*Shut your fucking mouth!*" Lovejoy screamed. His

nerves getting more frayed by the second. "I gotta call backup, and you're gonna stay right the fuck there, or I'll shoot you where you stand." His eyes then darted around as he looked for a telephone. Seeing one fallen on the floor next to a broken desk, he crouched. Keeping his aim and eyes locked on Jack, he blindly put his hand out to grab the phone.

Jack's eyes widened as he saw Lovejoy's hand miss where the phone was and, instead, land on something warm and sickly wet.

Lovejoy choked on his breath as he yanked his hand back, turned and saw what he had touched. There, a few inches from the fallen phone, Sally Noland's mangled, bloodied corpse lay. Buckled against the partition wall. In her hand, gripped in broken fingers, Matt Cordell's white glove, was stained red with her blood.

Immediately, Lovejoy screamed as he scrambled backward. His stomach lurched, and he could not hold back his vomit.

Seeing his chance, Jack broke into a sprint, running away from Lovejoy like the devil was at his heels, back toward the staircase he had come up from.

Lovejoy was in no state to try and stop him.

Teresa fell into Jack's arms as he got to her. The rain pouring on them as they stood beside the wrecked car.

"We gotta go now!" Jack said urgently as he kept an eye on his surroundings. "He could be anywhere."

"Frank . . ." she blubbed. Unable to say much more through the anguish.

"I know, but we have to go, okay? People are gonna come on duty soon, and they're gonna think *I* did this." Jack's gaze didn't look at Teresa once. He was too aware that, out of the shadows at any moment, the killer could appear. "We gotta go."

As the morning sun rose behind the beating storm clouds, Jack and Teresa ran as fast as they could away from the 14th Street Midtown South precinct. He led the way as they headed to the next block over, to Penn Station.

They both knew there was only one thing they could do.

They had to finish what Frank McCrae started, to take the Hudson Line to Sing Sing Correctional Facility and keep Frank's appointment with Dr. Felix Gruber.

Chapter 8

Over the one-hundred-three-minute train journey to Sing Sing, to Ossining, Jack and Teresa sat on their own in a shocked silence. They had each tried to come to terms with what had happened. What had happened to all those officers at the precinct. What was coming after them.

Jack could not shake the thought of his face plastered over every paper and television channel. Branded with the moniker of the Maniac Cop, with all those deaths, Ellen's death, being blamed solely on him. Every scenario he ran through in his head ended up the same exact way, him being gunned down before he even saw his day in court.

Teresa, meanwhile, knew that if she ran from this and laid low somewhere on her own, she may live to see 1988. And a few days ago, if she had thought about that for too long, she may have selfishly ended up leaving Jack to fend for himself, despite how much she loved him, out of sheer self-preservative fear. But not now. Not after Frank. Not after all the people Cordell murdered. This was bigger than her. Bigger than Jack. This was about stopping a maniac. This was about justice for all those people he stole the lives from. This is why she joined the force.

The train cut through the New York state landscape as the rainstorms started to dissipate, having emptied their payloads and drifted away to leave behind a cold, rising sun.

When the train pulled in at 7:10 a.m., the day had only just started. And as Jack and Teresa trod the twenty-minute path to the prison's visitors' entrance, they both looked far better than they should have. Teresa had put her hair up in a bun that hid how straggly it was, and Jack had stolen a blazer from a sleeping passenger, so he looked somewhat more respectable than him just wearing jeans and a T-shirt. Together, with a quick wash in the train station bathroom, they didn't appear like they had just escaped death; they just felt it.

"What can this guy tell us?" Jack asked as they approached the prison entrance. "Not like he can magic all of it away. It was a decade ago!"

"I really don't know," Teresa said, shrugging. "But Frank thought it could be important. Maybe there's more to this than we know? And the more we know, the more ammunition we have to clear your name and stop this."

Approaching the reception window, Teresa slipped Jack her police shield, then held back as he walked up to the stern-looking guard behind the bulletproof glass.

"I got a meeting with Doctor Gruber, but I forgot what time it was for," Jack flashed his most charming smile. "I think it was 8 a.m.? So, I'm a bit early."

The guard's expression remained stern.

"Name?"

Jack raised Teresa's shield to the glass. "McCrae. Detective Frank McCrae. I have my partner here as well, Officer Teresa Mallory."

The guard glanced over to Teresa, then back to Jack. He pointed behind them. "Go back round the corner. The doctor's office is outside the gate. You don't need to check in. It's the first two story building you get to. I have no idea when Gruber clocks in, but he should be soon, I guess."

Dr. Felix Gruber was a slight, wiry man in his early sixties, with an eccentric presence. With a mess of restless energy, he had a habit of licking his lips between words. This quirk, while innocuous, often became a focal point of attention, drawing people's eyes and leaving an impression of unease. His thinning hair, streaked with white, was wild and stuck out at all angles. He was a man who *was* his career and too preoccupied to concern himself with such trivialities as a hairbrush.

"Who are you?" he asked, staring at Teresa as she stood in his small wood-paneled office next to Jack.

"I'm Officer Mallory." She smiled nervously. "I'm working the case alongside Detective McCrae."

"Working the case?" he replied with a smirk, turning to Jack. "What happened to *just wanted a chat?* Now it's an investigation with this woman. Should I be nervous?"

"We just want to ask a few questions. That's all. Do you have a problem with Officer Mallory being here?"

"No," he replied, suddenly shocked. Realizing how his words had been taken. "I'm just not used to seeing many pretty women in here."

Jack motioned to the chairs in front of the doctor's desk. "Can we sit?"

Gruber nodded. "Please, yes."

After they sat, Teresa observed the fidgety doctor. She quickly noticed that he struggled to maintain eye contact. His gaze flitted around the room or landed just beyond her as he spoke. He was truly a man who did not enjoy any human interaction.

His reaction to her wasn't a sexist dismissal. He had the same issue with Jack. As the prison doctor, Dr. Gruber was accustomed to interacting with individuals who were either restrained, unconscious, or severely injured. His professional world left little room for conversation, especially with those who weren't part of his medical team.

"I'll cut right to it," Jack smiled. "You knew a prisoner by the name of Matthew Cordell back in '76, correct??"

"Cordell? I haven't heard that name for a quite a few years," Gruber said curiously. "But as to knew him? That's hardly the word for it. I performed the autopsy on that inmate. I remember that."

"I suppose you do a lot of autopsies?" Teresa asked.

Gruber looked slightly jittery by her question. "Is that part of the investigation? The number of deceased inmates I operate on." He licked his lip as he avoided her eye contact. "I have performed probably a hundred autopsies since 1976."

"Can I ask if his autopsy stood out to you? If there was anything unusual?" She added a polite smile as she talked, realizing that this doctor was on edge.

"Not many like Cordell," Gruber shrugged. "I remember it vividly, as it was so awful . . . He was slashed to death in the shower, you see? Never a nice way to go in here. But it's a common story. Over half of the inmates who lay on my slab for an autopsy landed here from some altercation with another inmate. Always stabbings. Sharpened toothbrushes, razor blades. I've even seen someone stabbed with a door handle." He sighed. "They use whatever they can get.

But Cordell was not just a shank to the guts like you'd expect . . . . No. It was far more brutal."

———

October 1976

The showers in Cellblock B were in a granite-lined room. Its gray walls were as cold as the air that crept in through the narrow, barred windows from high above. The chatter from the general population bled through the corridors and sounded like a distant hum within the shower room walls, interspersed with distant clangs of metal gates shutting somewhere in the facility.

The cracked, tiled floor that lined this room were perpetually damp from the showers being in use for most of the day, with the old, rusted heads almost always dripping.

Matthew Cordell had been in this prison for two months. He should have been in the protected custody block or in isolation but had found himself among the murderers and rapists he had thrown in here.

He would not allow himself to be afraid of this. The hand he had been dealt was a harsh, terrible one. But he would not hide. He never hid.

For someone like him, walking into a shower block was just as dangerous as anywhere else in the prison. So, no matter the situation, Cordell had to be on guard at all times. It was not like he could blend in. At seven-foot-one and built like a tank, he could hardly avoid standing out. He was so large people knew he was coming from a long way off.

He threw his towel over the stone partition of the shower cubicle, then stepped under the torrent of overly hot water cascading from the showerhead.

He could tell something was amiss. It was that time for him and the cells in his row to shower, but at ten minutes past 8 p.m., the rest of the cubicles were empty. He was the only one here.

But for Cordell, he would not worry or feel any nervousness. He would just carry on until he needed to act, would just—

A blade flashed out of the darkness from a neighboring cubicle, but Cordell's reflexes were faster. His massive hand clamped around the weapon midstrike, its razor edges cut into his palm. Ignoring this sharp sting, he wrenched the blade toward him with a brutal tug, dragging its wielder out of the shadows. The tattooed inmate let out a sharp yelp of pain as Cordell then twisted the blade sharply, immediately snapping the man's wrist with a crack. The bloodied weapon then clattered to the tiles, leaving the attacker screaming and clutching his mangled arm.

"You motherfucker!" the man cried in pained anger to him.

As Cordell stared down, his gigantic frame cast a shadow so big it swallowed the cowering attacker.

Though Cordell had quick reflexes, he did not see

the second, third, fourth, or fifth blades that suddenly shot out from the other cubicles toward him.

Toothbrush shanks, razor blades, cutlery, everything, was thrust at Cordell, before he even had a chance to turn to face them.

When the first sharpened edge of plastic split through his side and perforated his lung, Cordell felt a wave of numbness shoot through his torso, quickly followed by a terrible, burning pain. But he did not let that slow his response.

Immediately, he turned and grabbed the second attacker by the face, his huge hand almost wrapping around the man's head. With a defiant and furious scream, Cordell then slammed his hand toward the concrete wall, splitting open the man's head on impact. As this attacker fell to the floor, dead on impact, three more attacked. Hacking and slashing at his body with a brutal ferocity.

None of it slowed Cordell down, who swung devastating blows at the men. When his fists connected with their bodies or faces, it sent them flying back, bones cracking audibly with each punch. But when each one was downed, more attackers appeared from the darkness.

This was not an attack to teach a lesson as most prison beatings traditionally were. This was a coordinated assassination. And one that even Matthew Cordell, despite his violent efforts, could not beat.

The hacking and slashing then intensified.

Through skin, flesh, finger, and tendon, they sliced.

As his hamstring was cut in two from a low blow, Cordell fell to his knees, naked, bloody, and horribly wounded. The shower above him battled the blood that poured out of his wounds, cleaning them with their steaming water as it washed over him.

The agony through his body had become so great Cordell could no longer react. It had reached such an apex as every nerve screamed at him that he was silent, staring, wide-eyed. Unable to move.

The blades then came in again.

This time for his face.

"The authorities knew something like that could happen, right?" Jack asked. "Why didn't they protect him?"

"Who knows." Gruber shrugged. "The official word was that they did. That the warden tried to offer isolation. But the story went that Cordell refused. But I heard that the police chief at the time and the DA insisted he not be protected. Just a rumor, but still . . . Made more sense than him saying no to being safe."

"They made him?" Teresa asked. "That's more or less murder!"

"Personally, I believe he was condemned over the thought that any prison would allow their inmates say in where they are kept."

Teresa turned to Jack. "Wasn't Rook the DA in the seventies? Before becoming mayor?"

Jack shrugged. "Maybe, and I'd place money it was Pike who was the police chief." He turned to Gruber. "What do you do in a case like Cordell's, with his body?"

"What do you mean, what do I do?"

"When someone is all cut up like that . . . what's the autopsy for? You know how he died."

"Well, it's not like this is some ordinary mortician's business here. We're not into any cosmetic approach. So, we don't make them look pretty." Gruber sighed, still avoiding eye contact as he licked his lips. "When an inmate dies, it's not our job to make him look good again for the family. For someone who had been butchered to the extent that Matthew Cordell was, we just stitch the parts back together so he can be put into the wooden box in one piece. No finesse. Just function. And in his case, maybe autopsy was the wrong word. It was more of a reassembly." Gruber's voice dropped, his words spoken with grim detachment. "Cordell wasn't just 'cut up,' like you assume he would have been. He was annihilated."

For the first time, he looked at Jack and Teresa in turn as he spoke. "His cheek was hanging off, his nose nothing more than a fleshy pulp." He then held up his palm to them. "His hands were in pieces. He must have held them up to defend himself, but they were decimated. Fingers sliced off, bones crushed. They didn't even look like hands anymore." He averted his eyes again. "Bones broken. Stuck out in every direction. Neck snapped. Like they were not happy with him being dead, they wanted to punish every part of his body. And I do mean *every* part . . . So, for me as mortician it was not about finding answers. It's about making sure what's left is . . . recognizable and in one piece. We log every wound, every slash, every detail, for the record. It's paperwork. It's protocol. And for someone like Cordell, there's no dignity left to salvage. Just a report, a coffin, and a story no one will ever want to tell again." Gruber exhaled sharply as if expelling the heaviness of his words.

"What happened to the body?" Jack asked.

Gruber slowly stood and walked over to the bank of filing cabinets that lined his office walls. Looking at the small white labels on each drawer with years written on, he got to *1976* and pulled it open. After a few silent moments of rifling through manila folders, he pulled one out and opened it.

"Most of the inmates go to potter's field, as they've got no family would want to claim them . . ." His eyes searched the file until he found the information he was looking for. "As I thought, Cordell's body was claimed."

"Was it Sally Noland?" Jack said.

Gruber shot him a look and paused as he thought for a few seconds. He then closed the folder and walked back to his desk. "If you don't mind, would you mind showing me some identification? Something with your photograph on it?"

"Identification?" Jack said, hiding his sudden nerves at being caught.

"We'll be straight with you, Doctor," Teresa then cut in. "Detective Lieutenant McCrae died early this morning. He was murdered."

Jack stared at her, surprised by her confession.

She continued. "Murdered by the same man that killed over half a dozen people at police headquarters last night."

Gruber's face showed a glint of recognition as he sat at his desk, and he grabbed the morning paper from out of his open briefcase beside him. He swore he had seen something on the front page . . . Opening the paper up, he stared at the front-page headline that sat under a *Breaking News* banner: *MANIAC COP ESCAPES JAIL. 17 DEAD.*

He turned his gaze to Jack with a shocked stare. "Why are you really here?. How is this anything to do with a dead prisoner?"

"Don't bullshit us, Doc," Jack replied. "I think you know who did this. And the other Maniac Cop killings."

"How could I? I'm just a mortician!"

"Dr. Gruber," Teresa said firmly, "you know as well as we do that Matthew Cordell didn't die."

———

October 1976

In the mortuary operating room, Dr. Gruber had spent the last two hours stitching together the horrific wounds of Matthew Cordell.

Without much care, he had taken the heaviest gauged nylon sutures he could find and began piecing the man's body back together as best he could. Snapping bones back into place, closing the large open wounds. Pushing back the extruding intestines. It was a grotesque job but one Gruber could do on autopilot.

There were a few pieces that he could not save. One eyelid was missing. The man's nose was just mush of destroyed gristle. Various gashes could not be closed over properly, as there was no longer enough skin to cover the exposed flesh.

As Gruber worked on stitching the last wound up on this goliath's face as his fingers worked on the man's cold skin, he felt . . . something.

Did the man's cold skin twitch beneath his touch?

No.

Impossible.

Then again.

No.

No.

It can't be.

With an urgency, Gruber grabbed his stethoscope and put it over Cordell's chest. Listening intently for any movement from the man's heart. A heart Gruber had seen through exposed flesh only twenty minutes ago.

Then he heard it.

Faint. Weak but still there.

Thump, thump.

Thump, thump.

Thump, thump.

———

"We know he was not dead," Jack said, then pointed to Teresa. "She saw him. He attacked her. So, just tell us, for God's sake!"

Gruber looked at them with a nervous worry. "I . . ."

"This isn't us blaming you, Doctor," Teresa said. "We just have to know what we're up against. As much information as possible, so no one else dies."

Gruber nodded as he relented, knowing full well the truth would catch up eventually. "Look," he said. "He was a great policeman. Everybody knew, guards, doctors, all of us in here, knew that if we put him in with the prison community, he'd be attacked. I know the warden complained, but he was ordered. There was nothing anyone could do, and there was no way he could survive in there. It was not the prison's failing. It was those higher up who wanted Cordell dead. So, when he was brought in here and I found that pulse, I didn't tell anyone. If anyone found out, they would have probably have just put him back in gen pop to let them finish the job. So, I called the person who was down as his next of kin, that policewoman. Sally Noland."

"Why her?"

Gruber smiled nervously. "Why would I want to save a man I thought was wrongly imprisoned? *Why?* I was pissed off—if you really want to know. When I found out he was still alive—*barely* alive, mind you—I got angry that we allowed this to happen to a human, let alone a cop. And he was here, breathing, after all he had been subjected to? I needed to tell someone who wasn't part of this . . . And when she found out, she got me to do the decent thing."

"You let her take him out of here?"

"You have to understand, he wasn't up and at them," Gruber replied as he leaned forward. "He never *walked* out of here. And he wasn't *alive* alive. He had a pulse. That was it. It was weak at best. But I thought he would be dead in the week. If not sooner. And the brain damage the skull fractures would have given him—even if he woke—he would have been a vegetable. She took his body. But Matthew Cordell, for all intents and purposes, died in that shower block. He was just breathing meat sack who would never wake up again."

"But he *was* alive." Jack added.

"I'm *certain* he was legally dead. I wasn't really lying when I signed the death certificate. There was no way that Matt Cordell could ever function as a human being again."

"The newspaper paints a different story, Doc—"

Before Jack could finish, Gruber stood up and pointed to his door. "Please. I want you out of my office now. You never came here, okay? If asked, I have to deny everything. I'm not risking my career for this any more than I have already. It was a decade ago!"

Jack shook his head. "This is more important than your job."

"What did I do wrong? You should have seen him lying on that operating table, cut to pieces. I *knew* the system had screwed him. The politicians put him in jail, and the inmates did the rest. And now you're, what, going to ruin my life, my career? Over what? Over letting the man leave here when he was one foot in the grave?"

"We don't want to hurt your career," Teresa said. "We just need to stop him. Stop Matt Cordell."

Before they could say anymore, a nurse walked into Gruber's office unannounced.

"Oh, sorry. I didn't know you had visitors," she said with a smile.

"It's okay. They were just leaving," Gruber said. "How can I help?"

As the nurse walked over, Jack and Teresa looked at each other. With a knowing nod, they both stood and made their way toward the door.

"I brought you this to wear," the nurse said, taking

a green tie out from her pocket to Gruber. "It's Saint Patrick's Day, after all!"

Before they left the room, Teresa glanced over her shoulder, overhearing what was just said and a realization hit her.

Teresa and Jack walked at a hurried pace from the medical building toward the train station.

"The Saint Patrick's Day parade!" Teresa said. "Frank said one of the things he overheard at the pier was that Cordell wants revenge from the mayor and the commissioner. We have to warn them. They're both gonna be there out in the open."

"After what they did, part of me doesn't want to."

Teresa crinkled her nose. "We can't let it happen. We have to go there and tell them."

"Go there, along with five thousand other cops," Jack retorted. "I bet Cordell was one of those asshole cops that walked in that parade every year. Right at the front. For all to see. Loving the attention."

"You never walked it?"

"Oh, I walked it. At the back, pissed off I was having to dress up like a damn waiter in front of people."

Teresa couldn't disagree. The parade felt like an insult to most cops she knew. They spend their days trying to protect the very public who hated them.

Then, on that day, they had to wear their ceremonial uniforms and walk in file through the street.

To demonstrate our connection to the community we serve was the official line as to why they even got involved in the first place. Even though most of the NYPD were not of Irish heritage, that didn't stop the orders from above. They had to show up and march.

"But with a cop like Cordell?" Jack continued. "He musta loved that shit."

As they boarded the train back to the city, Jack felt a sinking feeling as he pictured the parade and the thousands of cops who would be there.

"They're gonna shoot as soon as I get there," he muttered.

The clatter of wood on asphalt echoed down Fifth Avenue as dozens of city workers hauled the barricades into place. The streets glistened under a crisp, chilly sun. Puddles reflected the fractured skies above, where streaks of blue broke through the lingering but empty storm clouds.

As a few early birds strolled along the avenue, bundled in heavy coats, vendors were already setting up their stalls on the sidewalks. Some offering coffee, some pretzels and hot dogs, all alongside a garish plethora of leprechaun hats and Irish flags, hoping to cash in on the festivities.

The parade was a couple of hours away, but the

street's energy was already building. Green and white bunting fluttered on lampposts, the festive mood a sharp contrast to the frantic activity at City Hall two miles south.

Inside that building, officials worked in overdrive, scrambling to secure the city since the discovery of the massacre the night before. Any other mayor would have canceled the parade, but having ordered "business as usual," the police and city officials worked in a panic to ensure the safety of the revelry on this—what was sure to be—a raucous day.

Unlike the rest of the city, the trash piles outside City Hall were absent. Unaffected by the sanitation worker strike. Here, it seemed like the city had no problem, which is just the way the mayor wanted it.

Jack stood across the street from the building, his baseball cap pulled down low, masking his face as best he could. He scanned the police and officials that milled around outside. Beside him, Teresa took in a deep breath, ready to go inside.

"What the hell do we tell them?" Jack asked, his voice low.

"I'll just walk in and say these killings are being committed by a dead man. Easy, right?" She forced a weak smile.

Jack shook his head. "C'mon, Cordell's alive. Gruber saw him."

"And I shot him," Teresa replied firmly. "Twice in

the skull. He's dead, Jack. I don't know how, but he is. I felt it."

"For Christ's sake, don't tell them any of that." Jack glanced toward the entrance. "Find Commissioner Pike. He'll listen. But no talk of zombies."

She frowned. "Where will you be?"

Jack nodded toward a bench in the park. "There. If you're not out by the time it all starts, I'll head to the reviewing stand on Fifth. That's where Cordell will go, for sure. Right where the important people sit."

"You'll go there? You'll be seen straight away!"

Jack shrugged. "If you don't get them to listen now, it's gonna be the only choice we got. If we wait till tomorrow, it could be too late. This is our best shot."

She hesitated, then kissed him before heading across the street toward City Hall.

Watching her go, Jack sank onto the bench. He wanted to run and just let Cordell show himself at the parade, let the world see what he was. But he couldn't. He was a cop and couldn't just switch that off.

Chapter 9

The door to Commissioner Pike's office swung open with a crash as Captain Ripley barreled in, his iron-tight grip on Teresa's arm as he dragged her in beside him.

"Look who was at reception asking to see you!" Ripley announced, his voice a mix of fury and triumph. "Jack Forrest's accomplice, Officer Teresa Mallory!"

Ripley thrust her in front of the desk like an offering. Teresa jerked her arm free from his grip as her bicep throbbed where his fingers had dug in. She spun to face him, her own anger risen to meet his.

"You touch me like that again and—"

"And you'll what?" Ripley shot back as he adjusted the stiff cuffs of his ceremonial uniform. "You'll complain to the commissioner or something?" His words dripped with mockery as Teresa's glare shifted to Pike, who, sitting behind his desk, had an unreadable expression. He leaned back slightly, his hands steepled in front of him as he silently judged her.

Ripley stepped back, creating just enough distance to give Teresa room to breathe. "We know you've been sleeping with Forrest," he said, his voice lower. "Frank's notebook spelled it all out for us. You remember Frank, don't you? The guy we had to scrape off his car after your boyfriend threw him out a window? Right in front of you? Yeah?"

The accusation stung. Teresa's fought to maintain her composure, but she could only picture Frank's dead, mangled face staring out of the wreckage at her.

"And we've got it *all* on camera," Ripley pressed, her silence spurring him on. "Saw you two running off together into the sunset."

Pike then finally spoke up. "The footage doesn't exactly help your case, Officer Mallory." His tone was casual but cold. "Running from the scene of a murder doesn't look great, does it?"

Teresa squared her shoulders, her mind racing to push back against the barrage of accusations. She took a deep breath in before she met Ripley's glare. "So, what you're saying is you have footage of us escaping the building? That's your big evidence?"

The room fell silent for a beat.

"Thought so," she said, her voice steely. "Yes, I broke Jack out. What you saw was us running from a killer. You saw us caught up in that horror. We had no choice but to run. And I'll tell you why. Because your department failed to protect Officer Forrest. You put him in custody during an investigation that made him a target, and you couldn't even keep him safe. That's *your* responsibility, not mine. I did what I had to do to keep your prisoner alive, and you know any court or tribunal will side with me on that."

Ripley's smirk faltered slightly, though his stance remained rigid.

Pike, meanwhile, raised an eyebrow. "Where is Forrest?"

"He's willing to turn himself in. But only if you're willing to listen."

Pike let out a low, humorless laugh. "Oh, so you're making demands?"

"I'm telling you the truth," Teresa answered firmly. "Jack didn't kill anyone. But I know who did. Someone *you* know."

Ripley folded his arms across his chest, leaning casually against the edge of the desk. "I'm dying to hear this one. So, who's the real killer? The mayor? The ghost of Frank McCrae? Gumby?"

Teresa's voice didn't waver through the sarcasm being leveled at her. "No. Officer Matthew Cordell," she said plainly.

The name hung in the air like a storm cloud. Pike's expression remained neutral, but the slight tightening of his jaw betrayed his reaction.

Ripley, however, let out a derisive snort. "Cordell? A ghost from the seventies?" His tone dripped with mockery. "Is that what you're going with now? Did you come up with this little bedtime story on your own, or did Forrest coach you?"

"It was McCrae's theory," Teresa snapped back. "You have his notes, don't you? The name's gonna be in there. And even if it isn't, we've verified it ourselves. Cordell is *alive*. And I not only saw him, I shot him. And he didn't go down."

Pike straightened slightly in his chair. "McCrae called me last night," he said, his voice quieter now. "He left a message on my machine . . . Would you like to hear it?"

Without waiting for a response, Pike reached across his desk and pressed a rewind on a tape recorder. When the reels stopped, he hit the playback button. The soft click of the machine was followed by the tinny crackle of a recorded voice.

"Commissioner," McCrae's voice began, rough and weary but steady. "I've uncovered evidence that the Maniac Cop has an accomplice inside the department. A female officer from midtown. I'm heading to Crime Records now. I'll call with more once I have confirmation."

The recording clicked off.

Pike leaned back in his chair. "Sounds like he was talking about you, doesn't it?"

Teresa's fists clenched at her sides with frustration. "You're desperate to close this case," she said. "You're so eager for a scapegoat that you're not even considering the facts. I'm not the accomplice. But I know who was . . . Sergeant Sally Noland. That's why Frank was going to the records library. Why else would he be going there?"

"Right," Ripley laughed. "Blame a dead woman. That's damn convenient, isn't it?"

His comment made her pause as she looked in turn at both of them, who stared back at her as if she was the murderer.

"The fact is," Pike said, "the log shows that you visited Jack Forrest in the lockup last night, on alleged police business. The suspect accused of being the Maniac Cop. Then you aided in his escape from that cell block. Probably helped him murder as well."

Pike then leaned across and pressed a buzzer on his desk. "We don't have time to listen to more nonsense," he said.

Almost immediately, Police Sergeant Fowler came walking through the door.

An older officer with a permanently serious expression came to a stop at the desk. "Yes, Commissioner?"

Pike waved his hand toward Teresa. "Get this woman out of my sight and into a cell. Place her under arrest. Accessory to murder in the first degree."

With a nod, Fowler turned to Theresa.

"Why are you doing this?" she said to Pike. "You *know* I'm telling the truth about Matt Cordell. You *know* Jack didn't do this."

Pike then stood from his desk, turned, and picked

up his police hat from the table behind him, along with his ceremonial white gloves. "I really don't have time for this," he sighed. "I have a parade to attend."

"There are going to be murders at that parade if you don't listen to me, *please!*" Teresa spoke franticly. "He's after you and the mayor."

Pike turned to her with a derisory glare. "Oh, is that what Forrest told you to say? A threat. If we don't let you go, we all die. Is that it?"

"If you have any sense, you'll stop the whole damn parade. Cancel it."

"Fifth Avenue's closed down. A quarter of a million spectators are lined up, not to mention the thousands of cops who'll be marching," Pike put his hat on before continuing. "And you think anyone is insane enough to try something? You have too much belief in your boyfriend."

Fowler approached Teresa with a pair of hand-cuffs, then grabbed her left wrist. "Hold still," he said as she slapped the cuff hard onto her.

She winced in pain as the metal hit her bone.

He then took the other cuff and manacled it to his own wrist. Tethering them together with a foot-long chain.

Teresa struggled, pulling her arm back. Fowler, though, was stronger and bigger and did not budge.

"Keep her on the premises for questioning," Ripley commanded. "I'll start her interrogation after the march."

Pike and Ripley then both turned for the door.

"Please," she begged. "I think he wants to kill right in front of the television cameras this time. He wants revenge for what you did to him!"

Pike looked back before leaving the room.

"Right," Pike said. "We know your friend Forrest and his MO. He's a lowlife coward. You know how we know that? He cuts the throats of lone victims in the middle of the night, when no one else is around. What you are saying is desperate and despicable and an insult to the victims. You should be *ashamed*!"

"Yeah," Ripley added.

Pike smiled. "If your boyfriend has any brains, he will steer clear of the parade. Then again, we know that's not the case. We shall have him in a cell beside you soon enough."

As they left, closing the door behind them, Fowler turned to Teresa with a look of curiosity, his expression equal parts intrigue as well as skepticism. Teresa, however, didn't meet his gaze back. Instead, she turned toward the window. The hand cuffs' chain went taut as she moved, yet there was just enough slack for her to lean toward the glass.

Through the faint glare of the window, she could see down as Commissioner Pike and Captain Ripley stepped into the sunlight and walked down the concrete steps. They moved with purpose toward a black limousine waiting for them at the curb.

Shifting her gaze slightly, she then spotted the

grassy area beyond the steps. There, sitting on the worn wooden bench, was Jack. His focus seemed to follow Pike and Ripley as they left. Teresa's heart sank. Jack's presence should have brought some semblance of hope, but instead, it just made her feel her own failure.

"Okay, I'm curious." Fowler's voice broke through her thoughts. His tone was lighter than she would have expected. "Why the hell did you both do it?" He stepped closer, tilting his head, as if searching for a crack in her armor. "I've seen you around. You seem like a good cop. So, lay it out for me . . . off the record." He let the words hang in the air for a moment. "Nothing you say can be used in evidence." A disarming smile played at the corners of his mouth as he believed his charm could loosen her tongue. "Was it for money or something? Me and some of the boys thought maybe it was a hit-for-hire deal. It's the only thing that makes sense to us. Something that could link all the victims."

Teresa turned to him. "Money had nothing to do with these murders. This is an act of revenge. Against the city. Against the mayor. And not by us!"

Fowler raised an eyebrow, his skepticism clear. "Come on," he said, amused. "You don't expect anyone to believe that, do you? They've got you banged to rights. You know that. You gotta spill the beans at some point. They'll make you crack within hours. Why not just make it easy on yourself and tell me the truth now? Save everyone the trouble."

Teresa's irritation deepened, and she let it show in her expression. "If I'm under arrest," she said flatly, "I'd like to talk to a lawyer. *Right now.*"

Fowler's smile dropped instantly, replaced by a more neutral, resigned expression. "Right, this way," he muttered. He motioned with his free hand toward a door at the back of the room. Without another word, he began leading her. Teresa had no choice but to follow as he dragged her along by the cuffs.

As he pushed the side door open, the hinges creaked softly. Before he could motion her to go through, a blur exploded into view, a flash of steel slicing through the air.

Before either could react, an arm lunged forward, holding a stiletto blade. It plunged directly into Fowler's chest. The force of which caused the hilt of the blade to crack against his ribs as the knife sank in as deep as it could go.

Fowler's eyes went wide as a strangled cry ripped from his throat. He staggered backward as blood spread rapidly across his uniform, pulling Teresa with him.

But he didn't collapse. Despite the mortal wound, he moved on immediate panicked instinct. His very survival driving him as he gasped in agony, turning, his face contorting in agony as blood erupted from his mouth. He used all his strength to bolt toward the main door of the commissioner's office.

Teresa, still cuffed to him, had no choice but to

follow, her steps stumbling to match his panicked retreat.

He stumbled through the doorway, dragging Teresa with him into the corridor as he fell forward and collapsed onto the linoleum below.

Teresa glanced back, her heart pounding as the Maniac Cop slowly walked across the commissioner's office toward them. So slow it was like he was playing with them.

She turned to Fowler in panic. "The key? Where's the key?" she asked, realizing she was tethered to a man who had no time left.

But Fowler could not say anything in response. He could only gag as his blood drowned his lungs and suffocated his breath.

The Maniac Cop was almost at the door, the knife in his hand. His pace still slow and deliberate.

She had no choice. She grabbed the dying Fowler and yanked him up to his feet. As she took his weight, he coughed, blood billowing out over his lips like vomit. Dragging him down the empty corridor, she moved him into the first office they came to just before Cordell stepped out of Pike's office to see where they went.

Inside the office, green crepe paper decorations hung from the ceiling, but there was no one around here. All the people had already left to go to the parade.

Lowering the almost dead Fowler to the floor in

front of her, Teresa franticly began to fish around his pockets, desperate to find a key to the handcuffs.

Before she could find them, the door behind almost smashed off its hinges as Cordell stormed into the room, knife raised, ready to kill. Glass and wood splintering and shattering around him.

In a terrified panic, she backed away, dragging Fowler's with her. Grabbing him by the wrist and pulling his weight along the floor and through an adjacent doorway. Fowler could not help. He was in his final moments.

Before Cordell could reach her, she turned and slammed the door between them shut, bolting it from her side. Not that the bolt could hold such a monster back.

She quickly turned back to Fowler, back to his pockets.

Then she realized what she had forgotten. She had her own key.

Grabbing her own keys from her pocket, she quickly unlocked the cuffs from her wrist. Just then, the glass in the door above her shattered, and the Maniac Cop was there again.

She knew, without having to think on it, that Cordell was playing with her. Toying with his prey. He could have caught up to her in the office. He could have got them in the corridor. But he was sadistically taking his time.

As the door cracked inward, Teresa lunged for a

nearby office chair, picked it up, and swung it behind her.

It cracked into pieces over Cordell's chest. The weight of it did not even stifle his pace. He just kept advancing, knife in hand.

"You're too late!" Teresa screamed as she backed away, her voice sharp and desperate. Her words tumbled out in a frantic rush as she looked anywhere for a route to escape. "They know who you are, Cordell!"

He then stopped in his tracks. Not because of what she said. But to stare down at the dying Fowler. It was only now she could clearly see the face of Matthew Cordell, the Maniac Cop. The light brightly illuminated his massacred face.

Fowler blearily stared back up in horror at Cordell.

"Cordell?" he gargled, recognizing the man in front of him, recognizing who this man used to be. He gasped for life as he said it again. "Matt Cordell?"

Without any reaction, Cordell suddenly raised his boot and brought it down with a violent force upon Fowler's head. Cracking his skull inward upon impact. His death brought forward by a few seconds in a grotesque act.

Teresa quickly spotted a large pair of scissors in among a pot of pens on the desk beside her. Grabbing them, she screamed as she attacked. After running forward, she plunged the metal blades into his chest, through his heart. She then pushed at him with all she had.

He staggered backward, peering down at the scissors handle that protruded from his chest. With his free hand, he grabbed it, then yanked the scissors out with ease, tossing them to the floor as he turned back to Teresa.

But she was gone.

The window behind her was wide open.

In the brief intervening moment after the attack, Teresa had managed to scurry out of the open window and onto the narrow ledge outside. A ledge which sat four stories above the ground below.

The ledge was barely wide enough for her to place her feet, but she had no choice. In those few seconds, she had escaped Cordell and pressed her back against the brickwork, inching herself sideways as fast as she could. She dared not look down, as the roar of traffic and the wind licking at her reminded her of how high she was and terrified her.

Just a few feet away, the metal of the building's fire escape beckoned.

Through the open window, Cordell leaned out to grab at her. But she was a few inches out of his reach.

Teresa pushed herself farther along, edging further from his grasp as he swiped at the empty air, closer and closer.

With no time to think, she lunged at the fire escape. Her arms stretched out as she threw herself over, her fingers just managing to grip the edge of its railing. The jarring impact as her body hit the metal frame stung sharply, but she held on tight, then desperately pulled herself onto the platform.

She clambered onto the descending ladder as fast as she could but could not stop herself from looking back up to the window she had escaped through.

It was empty.

Cordell was gone.

She eventually forced herself to tear her gaze away, turning instead to the street below. Down there, buses lined the curb as cops boarded in their dozens, all dressed in identical blue uniforms, ready to be taken to the parade. Others spilled out of the City Hall building, descending the steps in clusters. They joined the throng boarding, a mass of men and women whose identical appearances made them almost indistinguishable from one another.

Teresa's stomach sank as she realized Cordell could be among them. Despite his size, his grotesque visage, he could blend in among the sea of uniforms at least long enough to escape. No one would notice unless they turned to him. They would just see the blue of his uniform and hat.

Before she made to the ground, she peered across the grassed area, to the bench where Jack had been sitting.

He was gone.

He had left for the parade.

She then remembered Cordell's face. There in the office in a full unforgiving light. It was impossible to forget, no matter how much she wanted to.

It wasn't just grotesque. It was something far worse, like a living mask of horror, twisted by violence and hatred. His skin was pallid and sickly, almost gray in certain places, devoid of any life. Deep gashes and scars ran like fault lines across his skin, some jagged and uneven, others smooth yet thick, clumsily stitched together in places. His left cheek sagged slightly, marred by a patch of puckered, flaky skin. His mouth was twisted into a permanent, cruel grimace that was neither a smile nor a sneer but something far more unsettling. The lips, if they could still be called that, were thin, cracked and stretched unnaturally tight over his teeth, exposing a jagged yellowing row below.

A jagged scar crossed his forehead, running diagonally from his temple to just above what was left of his mangled nose, which was in ruin, cut off with a misshapen wound in its wake, the bridge exposed.

Beneath the harsh lighting of that encounter, she could see how Gruber had made a vague attempt at piecing his face back together into a semblance of humanity. But in that office, it was far short of human.

Even his hair—or what was left of it—contributed to the look as it poked beneath the rim of his hat. Sparse, uneven tufts stuck out from his scalp. Stringy, lifeless, emphasizing the mottled, deathly pallor of his skin.

The scars and damage had left parts of his face stiff and immobile, while other parts twitched involuntarily. A slight flare of the nostrils here, a twitch of the brow there, like his face was no longer entirely under his control.

But it was his eyes that haunted Teresa the most. They were mismatched in the worst way, one was sunken deep into the socket, its lid partially drooped from surrounding muscles giving way. The sclera stained with spidering veins of crimson and an iris that was a dull, lifeless brown. The other eye was even worse: it bulged unnaturally, wide and unblinking, its glassy surface gleaming with a faint, wet sheen that caught the light in the most horrific way.

Teresa's stomach churned as she thought of how close she had been to death. She blinked hard, trying to force the images away, but they clung to her psyche.

Around, the officers on the bus were in their own worlds, laughing, chatting, oblivious to the horrors that had happened within the building.

Teresa knew she had no choice. She had to get on one of the buses if she were to help Jack.

"Room for one more?" she asked as she looked up at the driver on an already packed bus, motioning to the police shield attached to her trouser belt.

The driver, also in uniform, looked at her civilian clothing curiously. "Bit underdressed, aren't ya?"

Teresa masked all her anxiety with a playful smile. "You try working vice all night, then be told you gotta make it across town for this shit."

"Oh, I hear ya," he replied, laughing. "We'll make room, squeeze aboard." He then raised his voice louder so that the nearest officers on board could hear. "I'm sure one of these animals will be gallant enough to offer their seat up to a lady."

With a thankful nod, she climbed onboard, the doors hissing loudly as they closed behind her.

Within moments, the bus had pulled away from City Hall and was making its journey north to the top of Fifth Avenue, at the start of the parade.

Having had a seat given up for her, Teresa was halfway down the bus by a window. Around her, the dozens of beat cops all complained about the march as they also spoke freely about how drunk they would get after, even though they were on duty.

Ignoring their banter, she just stared out at the city outside as the bus made its way up the parade route. Already thousands of spectators had descended en masse to Fifth Avenue and had begun to line the streets. Some were revelers dressed in white, green, and gold, some protesters holding signs up at the passing buses. Most had the initials A.C.A.M. daubed on them. A new acronym dreamed up by the press. *All Cops Are Maniacs.* As Teresa stared at the hate in the people's eyes, she could not hide her disgust in them. Every policeman she ever met put his or her life on the line every day. Facing off against drug dealers, rapists, murderers. Bad, bad people. Sure, a lot of the cops on beat may be brash, ill-tempered and uncouth. But who wouldn't be after confronting the filth of the city. Cordell was only one man, if he could even be called that. He was not the whole of the NYPD. A bad apple shouldn't condemn the orchard after all. But she understood their fear. She understood why they hated. She herself had seen the blinkered view of those in charge with this case. If Frank had survived, maybe they would have listened. Maybe if they were not so caught up in politics, the investigation would have had more than a small task force assigned to it.

The bus soon passed other marchers already lined up in orderly rows, their colorful attire bright in the morning light, while band members behind them tuned their instruments, ready to start playing. She also passed large floats made from papier-mâché and wood, all bright and garish, in the forms of anything even remotely Irish.

Hundreds of police had already arrived aboard the many other buses, clad in their pristine uniforms, and stood around, waiting, while others in regular beat uniforms worked on crowd control as they barked orders through bullhorns at anyone who pushed past the barricades.

"Back on the sidewalk! Keep the street clear!"

The commands rang out over. Even before the parade started, discounting everything with Matthew

Cordell, Teresa could feel a simmering to the day. As if tempers were going to boil over on both sides of the cordon.

Among the throng of onlookers, various camera crews from television stations could be seen recording segments for their coverage.

"Police are expecting the worst and special crowd-control units are stationed at strategic points along the parade route. Hundreds of people who've never attended a St. Patrick's Day parade before, some not even from New York, are here to protest the police. Angry that the Maniac Cop was caught, then escaped. The blame being put firmly at the NYPD as well as at the steps of city hall. This parade has always been a day of pride for the New York Police Department. But today, it seems that is more of a day of shame."

Through the crowd, with his stolen baseball cap pulled down, Jack Forrest kept an eye on the people around him. He for one was glad he was not in a uniform today as the angry voices he passed all spoke of how much they hated the cops.

Walking by vendors selling balloons, hot dogs as well as unlicensed stalls selling beer to anyone who had the cash, Jack tried to move fast toward the reviewing stand a couple of hundred feet ahead of him.

The strong smell of cooking meat did nothing to help this task as his stomach groaned in discomfort.

The last thing he ate was a bland lunch in his cell the day before. He just wanted to grab the food out of people's hand as he hurried on by. Ahead, he noticed that the stand was still empty. The commissioner, mayor, police chiefs and invited guests had not yet taken their seats.

Slowing down, he looked around. The parade was about to start. They *should* all be there. But the reviewing stand did not even have any chairs placed on it. It was just a vacant frame taking up space along the street.

Beside him, a squat, gruff man stood behind his stall, selling tchotchkes of leprechauns and other cheap St. Patrick's Day tat. He noticed Jack staring at the empty stand. "Fuckin' cowards, am I right?" he sneered in his gravelly New Jersey accent.

"Where's the mayor?" Jack asked.

The man coughed as he laughed. "You not heard? They're too shit scared to show their faces. Don't wanna face the crowds asking them questions."

Jack shouldn't really be surprised.

The man continued. "They're watching it all from a balcony of the Hotel Rockefeller. I'll say it again, fuckin' cowards, the lot of 'em. They'll get what's coming to 'em! A.C.A.M. Am I right?"

Jack smiled politely, nervous at the man's insinuations. If he knew Jack was a cop, that conversation would have gone in an entirely different way.

"They think they are safe up there," the man

added, with another lung rattling cough as he grabbed a half pack of cigarettes from his pocket and quickly threw one between his lips, then lit it.

Jack stared in the direction of the Hotel Rockefeller. He knew that, hidden away, they were still not safe. Not from the crowds but from Cordell. In fact, they were probably all more at risk if there were not a thousand sets of police eyes watching them.

Moving forward again through the bulging crowd, Jack narrowly missed hitting his head by a passing protest sign that read *Stop Marching! Catch Killers! A.C.A.M.*

A television newscaster, dressed in a green blazer with a white shirt and yellow tie, was standing in front of the Hotel Rockefeller. Around him, protesters could be seen with their signs as they shouted up at the hotel. Talking directly to camera, the newscaster spoke loudly into the microphone, ensuring he could be heard over the various angry chants. This footage was being beamed live to people's televisions.

"Because of security precautions, Mayor Rooke and other dignitaries will be reviewing this year's parade from the balconies at New York's new five star Hotel Rockefeller."

The newscaster's voice struggled over the crowd's increasing volume.

The camera then tilted upward and zoomed in on

one of the upper windows, where Mayor Rooke could be seen looking down at the crowd, waving at them.

"There he is now," the newscaster added. "Despite recently receiving the lowest approval rating of any New York City mayors, he's looking quite happy. Perhaps he doesn't see what the signs the protesters are holding say about him."

In the same shot, Pike sidled up beside the mayor on the balcony and whispered something in his ear.

The newscaster continued. "And there, beside him, we can see the police commissioner, possibly discussing the situation that is unfolding down here on Fifth Avenue."

The camera panned back down to the newscaster as he made his closing remarks of the segment. "In a moment, we'll return to our extended coverage of this seventy-fifth annual St. Patrick's Day parade. This is Burt Ballenbach for NYC90 News, back to you in the studio."

Chapter 10

Teresa's bus pulled to a stop alongside the reviewing stand on Fifth Avenue, one of the last police transports to arrive for the parade. Outside the bus windows, the parade was already in full swing, a vibrant, chaotic spectacle of color and sound. The dissatisfied rumbles from the crowd were temporarily muffled by the sounds of the marching band that played nearby.

After the bus's doors hissed and opened, the officers began disembarking one at a time, joining the sea of blue uniforms already gathered ahead, quickly falling into lines as they prepared to march.

Here, like at City Hall, it was not like the rest of New York City. There was no overflowing trash cans here or split bags leaking out its rancid contents. For today, the truth had been hidden for the sake of the parade. Instead, the air smelled of spilled beer, roasted peanuts, and the still-damp pavements. Not a trace of rot in sight or smell.

As Teresa stepped off the bus, an overwhelming wall of sound came hurtling toward her. The wailing from the marching bagpipe band was as piercing as it was deafening, and the drums that accompanied them beat a steady cracking and booming rhythm. This band marched steadily along, their kilts swaying in time with each step.

Further along the parade route, approaching St. Patrick's Cathedral, the crowd's restlessness intensified as wave after wave of police officers marched on. Angry voices rose above the noise, hurling insults without hesitation. Phrases like *March, murderers, march,* were screamed defiantly as every officer did their best to ignore them.

Within these onlookers, they were not all fixated on hate as a large number had come to support and see the spectacle of passing musicians, floats, and police. And those supporters did not appreciate the verbal violence that had been brought along to these celebrations. Soon, all along the parade route, infighting broke out among the crowd. The policemen working security tried to stop the fights, but as soon as they stepped up, all focus of hate got turned onto them so most of them stayed back and let the public sort out their own issues, only stepping in when the fights got too bloody.

. . .

In the Hotel Rockefeller, Mayor Rooke stood on the balcony of the grand penthouse suite. Draped along this balcony's railing, bunting decorations in the design of two flags, the stars and stripes and the Irish tricolor, fluttered softly in the breeze, a fitting—though quite cheap—tribute to the day's celebration.

Rooke was staring at Commissioner Pike in disbelief, aghast at what he had just been told.

"What the hell are you saying?" Rooke seethed in a whisper. "Cordell? What do you mean, Cordell? He's fucking dead! We made sure of that!"

"I thought so, too. But did we ever see a body?" Pike said calmly. "I didn't. Suppose he *is* alive, after all this time?" Pike leaned in as they continued to converse in hushed tones. "We have witnesses who say they saw him. McCrae sure believed Cordell was this Maniac Cop." Pike sighed. "It kind of makes sense if he survived. Who knows why he would wait so long, though."

Rooke regarded him furiously but tried his best to keep calm and for no one around them to see that anything was wrong. "I don't know why I let you talk me into throwing him to the wolves anyway." He grimaced. "I knew this would come to fuck us in the ass."

"What was the alternative?" Pike replied. "He saw too much. We had to offer up someone. Cordell was the best option. And it worked, didn't it? Him dying put the whole thing to bed, stopped any future questions of the people we sent him after and any missing money. They would just blame him. It was foolproof, and we got damn rich because of it. Right?"

"You sent your guard dog to the slaughter. A man who only did what you ordered him to! You can say it was to protect me or the city. But it was your ass you saved! Sure, he found out about the money we got, but we could have cut him in. Done something. Anything else."

"We're a bit too deep in this to be playing the blame game now." Pike spoke slowly and deliberately. "We both did what we did for our own asses, and it wasn't just us, remember?"

Rooke turned and glanced down at the parade, having reached the streets below. He forced a sudden smile as he noticed television cameras pointing up at him. "I'm not going to let it worry me," he said through his fake grin. "Nobody can touch us up here."

"Absolutely," Pike replied, nodding to the building opposite them. "Take a look up on that roof."

As Rooke looked over, he saw a collection of police SWAT marksmen lining the length of the building. Their long sniper rifles each had large silencer muzzles attached to their barrels. These continually traced the streets as the snipers stared through their sights, looking for any signs of trouble.

"We got the best marksmen on the force," Pike continued. "Over there and on the roof above us. Throughout the building. They've got us covered in all directions."

"What about this Forrester guy?" Rooke asked. "Who's he?"

"Forrest," Pike corrected. "He was the most likely suspect."

"And it's Cordell?"

"You think I'm gonna allow Cordell's name on the street? Not a chance. Forrest is the Maniac Cop now." He paused for a beat. "If Cordell is, in fact, alive and, for some reason, is doing all this to get to us, then we will deal with it when and if it happens."

"Okay, let's say it is Cordell, then why did he kill all those innocent people? Why attack the precinct. What has anything he done got to do with coming after us?"

Pike turned to the crowd below, the protesters, the placards, the fights breaking out, the dissent in their city. "For this. What better way than to turn the city against us, just like we turned the city against him? Even turn the cops against us for allowing it to happen to them as well. It may be extreme, but if that was the intent, it worked. It's like a powder keg out there waiting to explode."

Rooke, with a forced smile still on his face, placed one hand upon Pike's shoulder. "You know, my friend, if Cordell is alive and anyone finds out about any of it, you better start praying, 'cause I'm taking you down with me."

"And I'll do the same to you, too, Mayor," Pike replied with a sourer smile. "But that's a problem for tomorrow. Even if this maniac is Cordell, and somehow, he's out of prison and not in potter's field like we were assured, he never kills during daylight hours anyway. He only comes at night. So, we're fine here."

The parade moved on steadily as the drum majorettes passed below the balcony, twirling their batons with a timed precision, their beats soaring through the brisk air as they led the first band of brass instruments. Behind them, platoons of uniformed officers strode in perfect formation, in between large floats.

For a fleeting moment, it seemed as if the chaos of the moment had been left behind as the noise of footsteps, drums, and horns played out in a celebratory fashion.

Amid this spectacle, the undercurrent of tension remained as Jack pushed through the crowd of supporters and haters.

Unknown to him, on the opposite side of the street, a dozen meters back, Teresa had caught up, and she slipped between the parked cars and stalls lining the sidewalk. Her eyes too were locked on the looming hotel.

With the onlookers focusing their attention on the passing band, Jack moved fast, dipping his head whenever a fellow officer looked his watch, the brow of his cap hiding his face for a brief moment. But he was not invisible to everyone.

Across from him, a helmeted, armed officer spoke tersely into his walkie-talkie, his gaze fixed on Jack. "Alpha echo fourteen," he said. "Possible identification. Murder suspect Forrest heading through the crowd toward the hotel. East side of the street. Parallel to the crossing. Prepare to apprehend."

This officer's words set the machinery of law enforcement into motion. Other armed officers, their faces obscured by riot helmets, began to maneuver through the crowd from both sides of where Jack obliviously walked.

As they converged on his path, Teresa, nearer, saw this swirl of officers throughout the parade-goers. She then caught sight of Jack, saw what was about to happen, and was totally powerless to stop it.

The oppressive press of the crowd momentarily thinned around Jack as he got closer to the hotel, and he lifted his gaze up to the balcony.

On the balcony, a suited security guard stepped out of the hotel suite and over to Commissioner Pike. Leaning to his ear, the guard whispered something then left with a nod.

Pike stared down to the crowd, wide-eyed. "Forrest has been spotted in the crowd below."

"Should we step inside?" Rooke asked, also staring but had no idea what Jack looked like.

"We should stay here. It might not look good to let him run us off like that," Pike replied. "Gotta keep up the appearance, right?"

Rooke was not convinced. "As the kids nowadays say, 'you do you.'" He turned to walk back inside the suite, leaving Pike alone in the crowd's glare.

Jack, still unaware of his situation, climbed over a barricade, about to cross to the hotel, when a dozen guns came at him from all sides. On instinct, he held up his hands in surrender as the armed officers expertly closed in, surrounding their quarry.

"Hold it right there," the tactical squad leader said as he lowered his weapon to grab the cuffs from his utility belt. "Shake him down."

As he did one, another officer walked up behind Jack, then roughly and thoroughly padded him down for other weapons.

"You gotta take me up to see the mayor," Jack pleaded. "I'm not armed. You can have a gun to my balls if you want. But I gotta speak to him."

"Don't you go givin' orders," the squad leader sneered. "I ought to put a bullet right between your eyes in front of this whole damn crowd. And you know what? If I did, and they knew what you had done? They'd thank me for it. Probably even make *me* the mayor for doin' it."

Teresa watched this from the other side of the street. She could do nothing as she witnessed Jack get cuffed and hauled farther down. They led to a police custody van that was parked up, behind where the rows of news crews stood.

The squad leader picked up his walkie-talkie and clicked on the button before speaking. "Tell him that maniac cop is in custody."

As Pike was told the news, he looked down to the other side of the street and saw where Jack was being hauled into the back of the van.

"What fucking perfect timing!" he said, noticing the cameras, unable to hide his wide grin. "Nationwide coverage!"

Weaving her way between the police cars, Teresa wanted to cross over to get closer to the custody van, but the police closed off the area, leaving only room for the press cameras and the parade to pass in front of them.

"Sorry, ma'am. No one can cross," the armed officer had told her as she got closer.

"I'm an officer, not a ma'am," she said as she pulled out her badge.

"Either way, no can do," he said dismissively.

"Come on," Teresa said, her voice getting louder to be heard over the musical cacophony that marched by. "We're on the same side here."

The policeman shook his head. "Move along, ma'am," he replied, not wanting to give her any more of his time.

Deflated, she moved farther along the procession line to catch a better sight of Jack in the van.

A group of newspaper photographers and cameramen were at the barricade opposite, turned away from the hotel and pointing their lenses to the van, trying to get a glimpse through its small barred windows.

Suddenly, a young assistant looked back to the hotel. "The mayor's come back out!" he shouted as best he could over the passing furor.

Immediately, the cameramen turned their lens away from the van and up to the balcony of the hotel.

On all the news channels that were filming outside the hotel, all refaced their attention to the mayor, who took a stumbled as he walked out of the room. Falling forward, he grabbed the balcony railing. Most of these camera feeds were simultaneously appearing live on various stations, covering the parade in real time.

The mayor raised his hand above his head. A familiar gesture of a politician playing to the crowd.

"The mayor has come out again to wave to the crowds," one newscaster said, narrating the shot. "But . . . uhhh . . . he . . ."

They could not describe what they were seeing.

The mayor had raised his other hand, prompting the newscaster to comment. "He's waving to the crowd with both hands, just like Nixon. Though I doubt Mayor Rooke would appreciate *that* comparison."

But something was off with him. He didn't smile. He looked terrified.

In fact, the mayor wasn't waving at all. His movements were weak and trembling uncontrollably.

Before the gathered spectators or watching reporters could piece it together, his body was given a violent, uncontrollable jolt from behind.

Gasps rippled through the crowd as Rooke toppled over the edge of the balcony, with arms flailing. He tumbled down to the concrete and landed with a sickening thud in the midst of the parade below.

The music of the marching band gave way to the sound of instruments crashing to the concrete as the mayor's body slammed among the brass horns and bright uniforms.

The cheer of the moment was soon replaced by screams and sheer pandemonium, sending marchers and musicians fleeing in all directions.

The mayor's corpse lay sprawled in the middle of Fifth Avenue. His head, having taken the brunt of the impact, was split wide open. Jagged shards of skull bone jutted outward, surrounding the horrific cavity where the top of his head used to be, revealing the smashed brain matter within. A dark gush of blood spilled out from this massive wound and carried with it, pieces of grayish-pink matter.

His eyes, once commanding, had also been obliterated, crushed and burst from the violent impact. A terrible and horrifying sight to all those who stared at his body.

Instantly, the police had converged on the mayor, guns ready and aimed, following their line of sight up to the balcony from where he had fallen from.

Hurriedly, they grabbed his body and dragged it backward as other officers hurried the waiting floats by, getting them out of the street as quickly as possible.

The SWAT teams on the roof opposite the hotel were in a frenzy, as they had not seen anything through their scopes to alert them to any trouble. But each of them had their aim fixed at the penthouse suite, and they desperately scanned through the window, trying to see any cause of this terrible turn of events.

As their sights scanned the wide balcony, one of the sets of large glass doors leading to the suite suddenly exploded outward with a loud smash as a heavyset figure was hurled through it, sending shards raining down onto the parade.

The figure flailed wildly as the momentum carried the figure toward the railing. Slamming into it with bone-shaking force, his arms scrabbled for anything to anchor himself, managing only to find the fluttering bunting along the balcony's edge.

"It's the commissioner," one of the SWAT team announced.

"Anyone got eyes on the perp?" came the reply from his commander. "*Anyone?*"

For a moment, it seemed as though Pike might be able to hold on to the bunting. But the weight on the cheap decoration was too great. The railing groaned as the bunting soon tore and Commissioner Pike went over, bringing the string of American and Irish flags with him. He screamed as he fell, joining with the new screams from the crowd below.

The commissioner's descent ended with a sickening crash as he slammed into a float decorated by thousands of shamrocks. The force of his fall obliterated its flimsy construction, sending plywood and papier-mâché debris in all directions.

Leprechaun-costumed marchers, who, only moments earlier, had danced merrily on this float, were thrown like rag dolls onto to the pavement. Some sprawled motionless for a breathless instant before hurrying to their feet, panic in their eyes as they raced toward the safety of the curb.

Screams continued as spectators surged past the police cordon, shoving barriers and officers aside. The NYPD's attempts to contain the chaos were futile as shouted orders and waved batons only seemed to fuel the panic. The cheerful strains of bagpipes and the steady beat of marching drums had long since vanished, replaced by terror and confusion.

In the midst of it all, armed officers pushed their way toward the crumpled remains of the float. When they reached the heap where Commissioner Pike lay, they froze, horrified. His body, draped in the tattered flag bunting, was contorted amid the broken fragments of the float.

"Santa Maria, Mother of God," one officer whispered, crossing himself instinctively. His voice trembled as he leaned closer. "Are those . . . stab wounds?"

The others followed his gaze, recoiling as they counted dozens of puncture wounds across Pike's throat and chest.

Before they could move him, another eruption of panic swept through the crowd as the sharp snap of gunfire rang out from the penthouse above.

The SWAT marksmen searched through their sights into the suite as officers on the streets could only stare up helplessly.

But no one else came out.

Just the *bang, bang, bang* of gunfire, then . . . silence.

On the street, those that hadn't fled in fear froze as they stared, terrified, waiting for what could happen next or who else would be hurled over the side.

Through the hotel entrance at ground level, through the gleaming gold-framed glass doors, Detective Ripley staggered into view. His clothes were shredded and soaked in blood, the fabric clinging to his beaten body. One arm was visibly injured and bleeding profusely, cradled against his chest in a futile attempt to stem the flow, which dropped out thickly to the ground beneath him. Each step he took was heavier than the last until his legs buckled and he fell to the sidewalk.

A policeman nearby managed to catch Ripley as he collapsed. Gasping and trying to speak as his eyes fluttered on the edge of darkness, Ripley grabbed the policeman by the collar to pull him nearer.

As he gasped his last words, Teresa, also nearby, stepped closer as other officers gathered around.

"They thought he wouldn't come in daylight." Ripley coughed, wheezing and painful. "But . . . but he came. He got up there."

"Who was it?" The squad leader asked, making sure to constantly peer back to the hotel in case whomever it was had followed. But Ripley was struggling to breathe, let alone answer. "Who the hell was it?" the squad leader asked again.

"It was *him*," Ripley wheezed.

Teresa pushed by the officers and crouched beside him. Before the police could drag her away, she managed to steal Ripley's attention.

"You recognized him, didn't you? Even with all the scars? You knew who it was?" Teresa asked, not wanting to say the name herself, wanting him to admit what she had been warning.

"I'm sorry I didn't . . . Be-believe you," Ripley spluttered as his body began to tremble from blood loss.

"Who?" the squad leader pushed. "Who are you talking about?"

"Matthew Cordell," Ripley gasped as his eyes rolled back in his head, and he lost consciousness.

"Get the paramedic over here," one officer shouted. "We need to get him to a hospital *now!*"

Teresa stared at the hotel. She wondered how could a man the size of Cordell get into there unseen by all the armed guards—and not only that but had also managed to murder the mayor and commissioner.

"Right, clear by sectors, lobby first, then sweep to the upper floors," the squad leader commanded. "Secure all civilians and see if we can isolate the hostile. Expect resistance. Clear on my go. You and you, hold the perimeter for containment. Now . . . Go! Go! Go!"

As EMTs arrived and attended to Ripley, the armed officers held their guns up and stormed the hotel as a well-trained unit.

Teresa remembered. Jack. He must have seen out at all this from the metal confines of the custody van. She turned sharply, hoping to catch a glimpse of him at the small window.

The television crews remained fixated on the grim scene at the hotel entrance. They had completely forgotten about Jack. Teresa had to walk past them to get a clearer view.

She then caught an unsettling sight: a massive figure sliding into the driver's seat of the custody van. She knew who it was immediately and instinctively.

Her gaze locked onto the figure as it reached out for the driver's side door, then pulled it shut with a slam.

Inside the van, Jack's face appeared at the small window. His eyes wide in sudden alarm as the vehicle's engine roared to life. It then jerked backward violently. The sound of screeching tires cutting through the din of the crowd as the vehicle was slammed into reverse and sped out onto the street toward her, knocking down the wooden barricades, snapping them like twigs.

For the people who stood in its path and could not jump out of the way in time—police, EMTs, reporters and onlookers—were all smashed to the ground as they collided with the rear of the van, coming at them like a freight train, crushing them under its tires.

And it was speeding toward Teresa.

Managing to dive out of its path in time, she could only watch as the van pulled out into the center of the street, skid a U-turn, smash through another barricade, then race forward up Fifth Avenue.

In the back of the custody van, Jack felt as if he were caught in a violent washing machine as he was tossed around, battered with every jolt of the vehicle, without even a moment to steady himself. Each turn sent him flying, his body slamming into the opposite wall and steel benches with a thud. He reached out desperately to grab onto anything, but every time he did, the van swerved yet again, throwing him helplessly to the other side.

Up front, in the driver's seat, a pair of grotesquely scarred hands, caked in other people's dried blood, gripped the steering wheel. He didn't hesitate as he slammed the gas pedal down, crashing through obstacles and hurtling down narrow streets with a reckless abandon.

Outside the hotel, the scene had dissolved into utter chaos. Sirens wailed, drowning out the desperate shouts of officers who tried to restore order.

The police cars stood at a standstill as their lights flashed, trying to get through, to pursue the van. But they were trapped. In front of them, the wreckage of the festival float lay unmoved as EMTs darted through, struggling to reach the injured and the dead.

Amidst the confusion, camera crews jostled for the best angles, their microphones and lenses thrust into the madness to capture all they could. Shouts of panic and wails of fear only added to the confusion.

A newscaster stood stiffly in front of the camera. His voice was steady but tinged with urgency as though he were narrating the end of the world.

"Usually, a time of celebration and joy," he said

gravely, "the annual St. Patrick's Day parade has descended into unspeakable horror. The infamous killer known as the Maniac Cop has struck again, claiming the lives of the city's mayor, the police commissioner, and countless others in a brutal attack that has left everyone shocked and angry."

Behind him, the scene was anything but calm. The crowd, initially dazed by the violence, was seething with anger, their frustration directed squarely at the wall of police officers trying to hold them back. What had started as scattered protests had grown into a deafening roar of their fury. Men and women alike surged against the barricades, screaming insults and curses at the officers.

The police, visibly overwhelmed, tried in vain to contain this spiraling chaos. Their commands to "stay back" and "please go home" were lost in the noise, drowned out by the protesting voices.

If pressed, few in the crowd could have explained the source of their madness in rational terms. It wasn't a coherent protest or a targeted demand anymore, it was raw, primal, and all-consuming. They had been swept up in a cyclone of anger, a storm of emotions so powerful it obliterated any actual reason. Somehow, in the chaos of death and destruction, they saw the police as architects of their own downfall, the villains in a story where no logic lived.

The cameraman panned to the furious spectators, capturing the emotion of the moment: fists raised in the air, faces flushed with rage, tears mingling with shouts. As the newscaster continued his solemn report, the ferocity of the crowd continued, a palpable, unrelenting force that threatened to grow into something far worse.

Meanwhile, Teresa had bolted the scene, racing through the masses to the end of the crowd. It was here the line of police vehicles inched forward, their progress agonizingly slow. The sea of people were unwilling to part even for their blaring sirens and flashing lights. They just thumped on the cars with their fists and screamed through the windows at the officers within.

Teresa's eyes locked onto a familiar face behind the wheel of the lead patrol car. Captain Bremner. Her captain. Without hesitation, she sprinted toward the car, shoving past all those who stood in her way.

"Let me in," she screamed, banging on the car window.

Captain Bremner, head of the vice division, glanced at her sharply. His usual composed demeanor was gone, replaced by a nervous anger.

Without pausing, he leaned over and unlocked the door. Teresa, yanking it open, practically threw herself inside.

Moments earlier, Bremner had witnessed the van plow through the crowd outside the hotel, narrowly avoiding being hit himself as the killer made his escape. While others hesitated, caught between following protocol and ensuring their own safety, Bremner had made his choice. Throwing caution, and his own life, to the wind, he had rushed to his car and was determined to give chase.

"What are you doing here?" he gasped. "You shouldn't—"

"Please, just drive! We have to catch him!"

He shook his head but knew there was little time to argue. "Do you know how to handle a shotgun?" he asked, pointing to the one in the rack on the back seat.

"Just get close enough," Teresa replied, reaching back and grabbing the weapon as well as the box of shells from a container below them.

The next few minutes were a blur of chaos and adrenaline as Captain Bremner pushed the patrol car to its limits, weaving and barreling down the narrow city streets as its siren shrieked loudly and lights flashed. Teresa gripped the door handle as she braced herself against each sharp turn and sudden swerve, her other hand firmly on the loaded shotgun.

The city itself was an obstacle course, with dozens of police vehicles soon joining the hunt, snaking through the streets of lower and midtown Manhattan in an uncoordinated frenzy.

Officers tried to give updates over the radio as their voices crackled through bursts of static, relaying sightings and dead ends. Yet, despite the number of cars and the combined determination, the custody van remained lost among New York's urban sprawl.

As they drove, block after block, Bremner's frustration grew. "It's like trying to catch a ghost," he muttered.

Teresa scanned the streets ahead of them. The custody van's trail should have been easy to follow. It had left destruction in its wake, smashing through anything and anyone in its path. But the overflowing trash that lined every sidewalk, spilling their refuse into the gutters, made it impossible to differentiate fresh debris from the destruction left by the vehicle.

"Didn't *anyone* see which way it went?" Teresa asked, her voice tense with disbelief.

"Some said it was at the East Village, others Soho," he replied through gritted teeth. "No one's thinking straight."

"They must have had a plan. Whoever's driving that van, they're not just fleeing blindly. They knew the chaos would buy them time."

The radio crackled to life. A voice shouted, "Possible sighting near Bowery and Houston. Unit in pursuit."

As Bremner was about to slam on the gas to follow, Teresa reached out and grabbed his hand.

"Wait," she said urgently, remembering what Frank McCrae had told her. "I think I know where he could have gone."

"What? Where?"

"Pier 14," she replied.

"What do you know?" Bremner looked at her curiously.

The radio crackled to life again. "False Alarm. Standing down," the officer said with disappointment.

"Please, trust me. What have we got to lose?"

Chapter 11

Pier 14 sat in the cold spring sunlight, its skeletal frame a grim monument to decay, looking like the shipwreck stranded on a shore. An abandoned ruin of rotten planks and corroding metal precariously sitting above the sluggish waters of the Hudson.

In daylight, the truth of Pier 14's abandonment was clear. Unlike in the shadow of night, when Detective Frank McCrae had last walked this ground, the large, sun-faded sign declaring *CONDEMNED FOR DEMOLITION* was unmissable. Plastered on the chain-link fences that surrounded the area and tacked haphazardly onto the peeling facade of the main building, there was no doubt of the condition of the structure.

Through the open gate, in the middle of the large decaying warehouse, amid the debris and filth left strewn around, the custody van was parked.

Inside this wagon, Jack still sat, his eyes darting to the grim view outside the tiny window. His body ached after being hurled about on the frantic journey here and was covered in bruises yet to appear. He could see he was at a pier but had no idea why.

The heavy slam of a driver's door broke through the silence like a thunderclap. Jack's head snapped around to look out the other window. Through it, he saw the towering figure emerge from the cab. He had never seen this man till now, but Jack knew, even through this snatched glance, that it was Matthew Cordell, the Maniac Cop. As he passed by the window, his broad frame cast a shadow that swallowed the light and sent a fleeting darkness over Jack's scared face.

As Cordell walked, his billy club was spun effortlessly in his monstrous hand. The movement unnervingly hypnotic: it snapped back into his palm with a crack, only to spin around his wrist again and be caught deftly on the other side, then all back again. A relentless rhythm. *Crack, spin, crack.* One that turned Jack's stomach as he heard it, even not knowing what the sound was from.

Jack moved to the rear of the van and peered out the back window, trying to see where Cordell was walking to. But like an apparition, he seemed to have disappeared. All that lay outside was the dilapidated and damp warehouse.

He exhaled a small sigh of relief—not that there was much to be relieved about. He was still locked in the van with no means of escape, but Cordell seemed to have left.

But then something appeared at the window. Recoiling, Jack could not contain his scream as he came face-to-face with Matthew Cordell staring in. His mottled flesh, lacerated face, stretched skin over his cracked teeth, one sunken and one bulging eye, all made Jack feel both sick and terrified as he backed away. The image of what he looked like in Jack's imagination was so much worse in the flesh.

The broken face then moved from the window as Cordell grabbed the handle to the doors and tried to open them, but they were locked. Dead bolted to keep the prisoner safely inside and unable to be broken out without the keys.

In fury, Cordell let go of the handle and began to pound his fists upon the door like a silverback. He hit them with such a force that the entire vehicle shook from side-to-side. The sound inside was a deafening reverberating boom. Each hit slammed on the toughened steel doors with such strength, that not only did the noise hurt to hear but the metal it was made from began to buckle inward.

"*Cordell!*" Jack screamed, trying to get the monster's attention. "You've done it. You've killed the guys who put you away. It's over. You can stop now."

Then, as if listening, the pounding suddenly ceased. The door bent slightly in but still holding firm, able to keep the Maniac Cop out.

Jack, thinking he had got through to the man, edged closer to the door. "You don't have to kill anymore," he said loudly. "You won!" But as he spoke, he looked out of the window and expected to see Cordell standing there.

But he had disappeared again.

Affixed to the wall by the entrance to the warehouse building, an aged leaky fire extinguisher hung next to a coiled rotten hose on a metal spindle. The rusted fire ax that had been hanging there was missing.

Jack, presuming Cordell had left the pier, hurriedly traced his fingers around the doors, hoping to find a way to open them from the inside. He could not see much despite the light that crept in through the three barred windows, as the shadows inside were heavy and stubborn. Even the new, thin gaps by the edges of the door, the ones opened by the barrage they had just endured, only let through the murkiest of beams.

Smash.

A fire ax slammed into the door, narrowly missing Jack's finger as he felt for any escape. The sheer power of the swing sent the rusted edge into the steel door with ease.

Then another swing. The blade careened through

the air and smashed into the lock on the door, crumpling it inward.

Another.

Then another.

Then another.

One after the other, the ax swung at the door, its head embedding in the metal with each swing, creating a jagged hole to the outside before being pulled back out for another round.

All Jack could do is stand there, dreading the violence that was heading toward him.

"The gate's open," Teresa exclaimed, pointing to the entrance to Pier 14 as they pulled up in the patrol car, the lights still flashing but the siren quiet.

Captain Bremner was not convinced by any of this. Stopping the car, he looked out of the windshield at the warehouse building ahead. Everything seemed still. Nothing seemed wrong.

"Probably just vandals breaking in or something," he said dismissively.

"Come on," Teresa said as she opened the car door and, grabbing her shotgun, got out. All the while keeping her gaze ahead.

Not knowing what else they could possibly do, Bremner grabbed a second shotgun from the back seat and, after fully loading it, got out to join her.

"Are you sure this is where Frank went?" he asked, keeping his volume in check.

Teresa nodded.

"What's the plan, then?"

"You call in backup," Teresa said. "I'll see if I can see anything in there."

"Okay, but if in the slim chance you do see anything, don't engage. Come back out."

Teresa did not listen to that last command. She just started walking through the gates, her shotgun at her hip, toward the warehouse. As she got nearer, she started to hear it. *Smash, smash, smash.*

The sound of steel on steel.

The doors to the van finally gave way from the attack met upon them. They twisted inward, breaking off their hinges with a deafening crash, threatening to fall onto Jack, but he flung himself against the wall of the wagon, narrowly avoiding their jagged remains.

Through the broken doorway, Jack saw him.

Cordell.

The hulking, malevolent figure, ax in hand, was staring right back at him.

Jack didn't wait. He could not afford himself the luxury, not with his life on the line. With a desperate cry, he launched himself out of the van, with every ounce of his weight propelling him like a battering ram.

His impact against the Maniac Cop was intense, born of terror and survival instinct.

This momentum knocked Cordell off balance as they both went crashing down onto the pier's wooden floorboards.

Jack didn't waste a second as he clambered to his feet and seized the ax that had fallen from Cordell's grasp.

Turning back, Cordell was also on his feet, advancing on him with his hands outstretched, grasping.

Savagely, Jack swung the ax at Cordell's side. The blade sank into his waist with a meaty thud. But there was no scream. No spray of blood. No contortion of his body, just an eerie, empty stillness as though the weapon had struck stone.

Cordell then turned, his mutilated face displaying no emotion and swung his arm, swatting Jack aside with ease.

He went skidding across the rotten floorboards as Cordell monstrously followed to carry on his assault.

Jack could see every grotesque detail of this maniac cop as he approached. His cold, unfeeling eyes stared as his scarred hands grabbed his billy club from his utility belt and unscrewed the end. The glint of the concealed stiletto blade then came into view.

Cordell raised this weapon high as Jack scrambled, but the monster was on him. He seized Jack by the throat and lifted him. His strength was inhuman as he held him high on one hand, the blade ready to strike with the other. No matter how frantically Jack's struggled, it was useless against this beast.

The knife's point hovered inches from Jack's throat as the almighty sound of a shotgun blasting caught them both off guard.

The shot hit Cordell in the shoulder, causing him to lose grip of the knife. He turned to see where this attack was coming from.

Teresa, shotgun in hand, came rushing forward as she opened up another blast, hitting Cordell in the back. He immediately lost his grip on Jack, who fell to the ground, choking.

She then grabbed a handful of new shells from her pocket and started to reload her weapon as Cordell, like a machine, stood again. The injuries on his shoulder and back were bloodless. They were pale, fleshy wounds that did nothing to slow down his movements.

Almost upon her, she managed to reload in time and turned the gun on Cordell, firing point-blank into his chest.

Cordell staggered backward a step as the shot hit, tearing through his uniform and into his cold flesh. He did not stop, though, as he continued again toward her.

She tried to fire off another shot, but he smashed the shotgun from her grasp. He then reached out, but before he could grab her, Jack jumped into the melee, ax in hand. He swung it into Cordell's back. Burying it deep into his shoulder blade.

Still no blood or cries of agony, Cordell reached over his shoulder, grabbed the ax, ripped it out, and dropped it, all while fixing his stare on them.

With the Maniac Cop standing in between them and the exit, Jack and Teresa hurried in the opposite direction. Running around the rotten crates and piled up debris, they hoped to find a side door. But their escape route soon came to an abrupt halt as they found themselves at the loading end of the warehouse. This whole end of the building was open to the elements. The floorboards ended, leading to a sheer drop, down into the dark churning waters of the river.

As they stood, not knowing what to do, the rotten wood beneath their feet groaned and creaked. Barely strong enough to sustain their weight.

They needed to turn and run back into the warehouse, but Cordell was storming toward them, knife still in hand, blocking their only direction.

"Hey, freeze!" Detective Bremner shouted as he appeared from behind Cordell. Shotgun aimed at his back.

"It won't do any good!" Theresa shouted. "Run!"

"I got this, little lady." Bremner smirked.

Cordell had stopped in his tracks and turned, staring at this new arrival.

"You have the right to remain silent," Bremner

added, walking toward Cordell. But before he could say anything else, Cordell sliced at him with his knife.

Bremner didn't have a chance to pull the trigger as the stiletto blade ripped through his neck, viciously tearing through his throat. Before he could collapse, Cordell turned the knife back and sliced the other way, decapitating him in two quick moves.

Teresa and Jack stared in shock as Cordell picked up Bremner's shotgun with his free hand and turned back to them.

They were stuck.

This homicidal maniac ahead of them, the thunderous currents of the river behind them.

In the distance, a multitude of police siren screams drifted through the air. Help was getting closer with every second, but they were still too far away.

"Hey," Jack called out. Hoping he could connect with the monster. "You hear me?"

"Matt?" Teresa added.

Upon hearing his forename, Cordell stopped in his tracks as if hearing their words for the very first time.

"What do we say?" Jack whispered.

Teresa shook her head. She had no idea.

"Matt?" Jack added, taking up Teresa's approach. Speaking off-the-cuff. "Listen. This was *your* city, right? You gave your life to protect it from the bad people. Didn't you?"

Cordell stared at them. Listening.

Jack continued, having no idea what he was saying.

"But there's another bad person going around, killing innocent people. Wouldn't you have just taken those people outside and sentenced them yourself? Those scum would probably get let off on a technicality if you just arrested them, right?"

Cordell's head slowly dipped as if he was thinking, but there was no expression. No sound.

"Those scum don't deserve a jury. And this guy, he's guilty as well, right?"

Teresa stared at Jack, unsure of what he was doing but stood in awe that it, somehow, was working. That Jack was confusing Cordell enough to stop him.

"Matt, don't let this guy kill us," Jack said. "We're innocent people. We're not criminals. Hell, both of us are cops just like you."

Slowly, Cordell raised the shotgun.

"Oh no," Teresa whispered fearfully.

But the gun did not aim at them. It moved up and came to a stop under Cordell's chin.

"Matt, do it!" Jack shouted. "Save us!"

"Is this really working?" Teresa whispered to Jack.

The next couple of second stretched out as they both waited for Matt to punish the Maniac Cop the only way he knew how.

But that shot never came as a small grimace spread over his mangled face, and the shotgun was brought back down again, leveling straight at them again.

Jack's shoulders sank as he mumbled. "Guess, no, it didn't work."

Cordell understood what they were saying, but the monster inside was too great, too mad, too murderous to stop. He then took a step forward, and as he did, the floorboards beneath him creaked under his immense weight.

The next creaked even louder. He was stepping on the more rotten, weather damaged boards.

Noticing this, Jack turned to Teresa with a nervous smile. Before he could second guess his actions, he hurled himself toward Cordell. As he landed in front of the Maniac Cop, the combined weight of their struggle proved too much for the already strained floorboards.

The damp wood groaned, cracked and creaked louder and louder until they finally gave way with a sharp crack. Both men plummeted through the shattered wood toward the river far below.

Down the hole beneath them, the waters churned around a dozen rotted pilings, their jagged, splintered tips resembling the spikes of a brutal animal trap.

As they began to fall through, Teresa rushed to the edge and, thrusting her arm out toward Jack, managed to catch his hand, stopping his descent just in time.

Cordell, however, was not as fortunate.

He fell backward, down to the water, and hit the pilings with a sickening force. The decayed wood pierced through his body, bursting bloodlessly through his back and emerging through his chest. As he writhed, trying to break free, his gargantuan efforts only drove the stakes further into his body.

The further he was impaled, the more his body jerked ferociously against it. The power of his thrusts soon started to tear the pilings from their moorings beneath him. As each one snapped off, his body began to sink further. All with no screams or noise from his twisted mouth. With one last effort, before he went beneath the water, Cordell reached up, his enormous hand swiping at Jack's dangling leg, intent on dragging him down. But the lunge fell short as the last piling snapped off, the weight of the wood impaling him and pulling him under.

Teresa, summoning every ounce of strength she had left, managed to pull Jack back up through the hole.

Sat on the edge of the broken floorboards, they did not know what to say to each other as they stared into each other's eyes, gasping for breath.

After a few moments, they staggered to their feet, and Jack noticed something glinting at the edge of the collapsed planks. Something silver, a police badge. Cordell's police badge. It had fallen from his uniform in the scuffle.

With a smirk, Jack bent down to pick it up, probably the only evidence they would have that any of this happened.

But before he could turn to show Teresa what he had found, a sudden crash erupted up through the floor. With an immense fury, Cordell surged upward, his head, shoulders and massive arms bursting through the decaying floorboards. Though still impaled by the long pilings, he reached madly at Jack, his expression no longer blank but filled with fury.

Teresa reached out and pulled Jack toward her, away from Cordell's murderous grasp.

But as Cordell came up, the weight of his own body and the impaled pilings dragged him back in, crashing into the waters below. This time, the depths swallowed him completely, leaving nothing but ripples on the surface.

A multitude of police sirens screamed through the streets.

As cars and vans screeched through the gates of Pier 14, armed officers leaped from their vehicles, weapons drawn and ready for confrontation. But their determined bravado quickly gave way to disbelief as they saw Jack and Teresa slumped outside on the ground, utterly exhausted yet visibly relieved.

"Where is he?" a police sergeant asked.

"At the bottom of the river, I guess," Teresa answered, too mentally tired to think.

"You know who it was?"

Jack looked up at the sergeant and handed him Cordell's police badge. "You figure it out," he said, not wanting to have to go through that question yet again.

. . .

The police and forensic investigators methodically combed through Pier 14, sending divers into the murky depths in search of a body. But they found nothing.

"The current would've dragged him downstream," one diver informed the lead detectives grimly. "Probably took him out to sea. We may never find a body or be able to identify him."

The team had also taken fingerprints from the van, hoping to uncover the killer's identity. What they discovered only deepened the mystery: the prints belonged to Matthew Cordell. A man long dead.

When splintered pilings washed up farther down-river, smeared with what appeared to be chunks of decayed flesh, the investigators were left baffled. The grotesque discovery did nothing to clarify the case; instead, it stoked the flames of an urban legend, fueling whispers of the Maniac Cop rising from the grave to exact his vengeance.

Ultimately, the case was closed with a plausible yet unsatisfying conclusion: the so-called Maniac Cop was an unidentified serial killer posing as the late Matthew Cordell. Official reports lauded Officers Forrest and Mallory as heroes, crediting their bravery in stopping the murderer. They were even awarded medals for their services to the city. All traces of Jack's arrest scrubbed from the records.

Funerals for the slain officers and civilians were

marked with grandeur as tributes poured in from the new mayor and dignitaries alike. Each eulogy reflected the bravery of those lost, leaving the city both mournful and mystified, with the shadow of the Maniac Cop lingering in its collective memories.

The storms soon returned to the city. Drenching the city in forked lightning and tropical downfalls.

No one was at Pier 14 to witness what rose up from the depths of the waters, from below the tangle of moss and debris that littered the riverbed.

No one saw the hand, immense, gnarled and hideously scarred, emerge from the depths and grip the side of a broken piling.

No one saw and realized that the dead can never truly die.

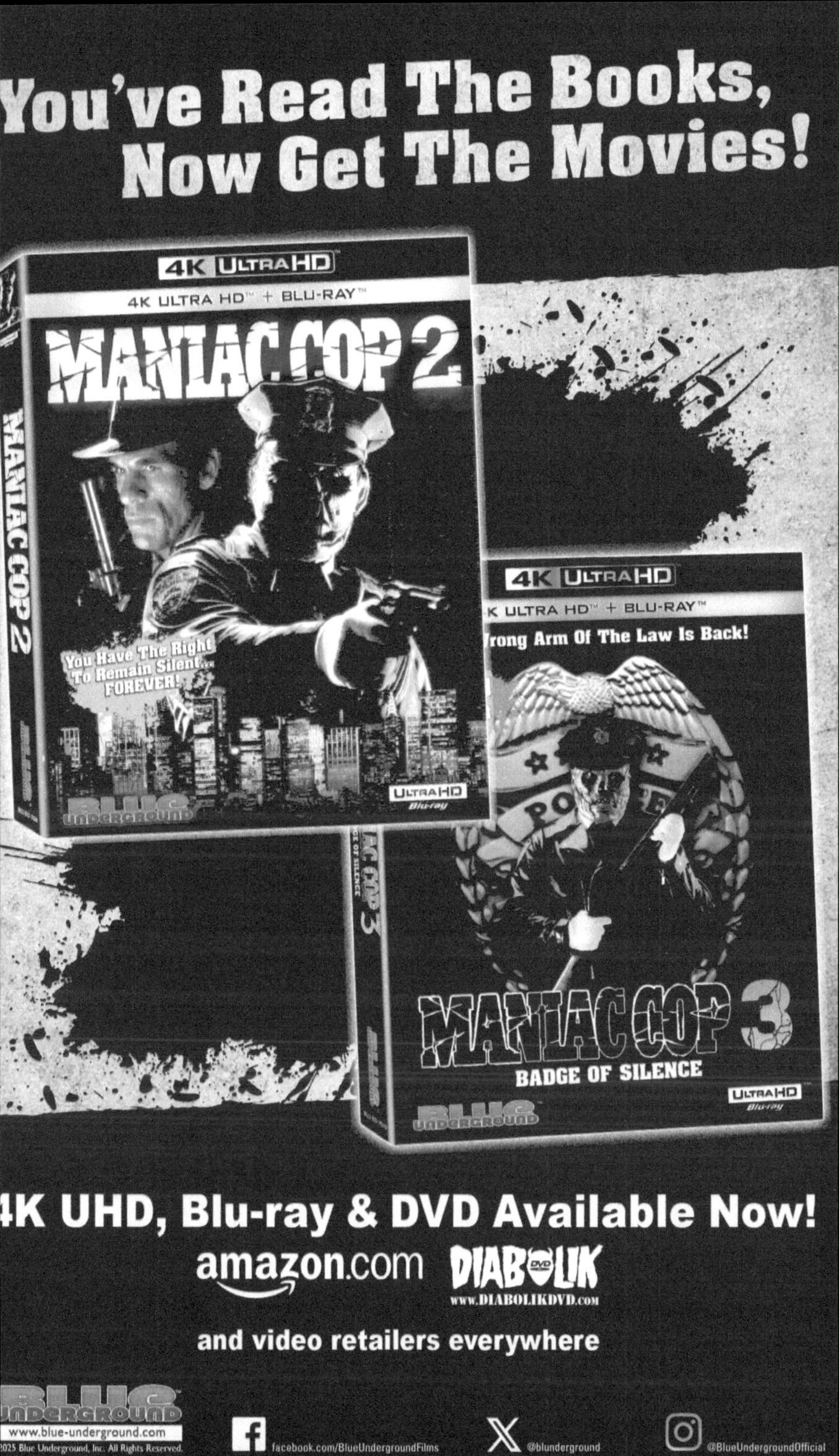

You've Read The Books, Now Get The Movies!

4K UHD, Blu-ray & DVD Available Now!

amazon.com DIABOLIK
www.DIABOLIKDVD.com

and video retailers everywhere

Also by Christian Francis

Official Novelizations

Session 9: The Official Novelization

978-1-916582-59-0 (eBook)

978-1-916582-60-6 (Paperback)

978-1-916582-61-3 (Hardcover)

Released October 2024

★★★★★

"This book was a WILD ride. I was literally biting my nails while getting through it!"

Skylere K (Netgalley)

The First Power: The Official Novelization

978-1-916582-95-8 (eBook)

978-1-916582-66-8 (Paperback)

978-1-916582-67-5 (Hardcover)

Released April 2025

Maniac Cop

978-1-916582-68-2 (eBook)

978-1-916582-70-5 (Paperback)

Released May 20 2025

Maniac Cop 2

978-1-916582-71-2 (eBook)

978-1-916582-73-6 (Paperback)

Released May 20 2025

Maniac Cop 3

978-1-916582-74-3 (eBook)

978-1-916582-76-7 (Paperback)

Released May 20 2025

Maniac Cop Trilogy

978-1-916582-69-9 (Hardcover)

978-1-916582-72-9 (Mass Market Paperback)

Released May 20 2025

From Echo On Publications

- The Gate (*coming soon*)
- Dee Snider's Strangeland (*coming soon*)
- 3615 Code Père Noël aka Deadly Games (*coming soon*)
- In The Mouth of Madness (*coming soon*)

plus many more to be announced.

From Titan Publishing Group

- The Descent (*coming soon*)

From Encyclopocalypse Publications

- Wishmaster
- Vamp
- Creature, aka Titan Find

Original Novels and Novellas

The Dead Woods

YA Horror

978-1-916582-00-2 (eBook)

978-1-916582-02-6 (Paperback)

978-1-916582-04-0 (Hardcover)

★★★★★

"One of the best YA books I have ever read."

David W Adams (Amazon)

———

The Devil and The Deep

Cosmic Horror

978-1-916582-52-1 (eBook)

978-1-916582-55-2 (Paperback)

978-1-916582-54-5 (Hardcover)

The Sacrifice of Anton Stacey

Horror Novella

978-1-916582-06-4 (eBook)

979-8-386183-59-2 (Paperback)

Everyday Monsters - The Animus Chronicles 1

Dark Fantasy / Horror

978-1-916582-03-3 (eBook)

978-1-916582-09-5 (Paperback)

978-1-916582-10-1 (Hardcover)

Incubus: The Descent - The Animus Chronicles 2

Dark Fantasy / Horror

978-1-916582-08-8 (eBook)

978-1-916582-11-8 (Paperback)

978-1-916582-12-5 (Hardcover)

Anti Rule: Navigating The Lies About Fiction Writing

Non-Fiction

978-1-916582-01-9 (eBook)

978-1-916582-05-7 (Paperback)